DETERMINED IN ALL WORLDS

A Novella

By J W Voyce

ISBN 9798530133909

Cover image
Copyright © Clarisse Meyer
www.unsplash.com

Cover design
Copyright © 2021 J W Voyce

"Whether or not it is clear to you,
no doubt the universe is unfolding
as it should."

Max Ehrmann

Desiderata: A Poem for a Way of Life

"Everything is determined, the beginning as well as the end, by forces over which we have no control. It is determined for the insect, as well as for the star. Human beings, vegetables, or cosmic dust, we all dance to a mysterious tune, intoned in the distance by an invisible piper."

Albert Einstein

"A moment or two of serious self-scrutiny, and you might observe that you no more decide the next thought you think than the next thought I write."

Sam Harris

Free Will

YouTube.com/ResonantTales

Visit for free short stories narrated by the author.

Instagram @jwvoyce

Facebook /ResonantTales

For Karen Voyce, Ben Millane, and Catherine Leng,
whose support and encouragement will always be treasured.

April 3, 1997

'You can have it back when you say, "Peter Piper picked a peck of pickled peppers".'

Tyra's recital of the line was enviably fast, and the encircling group roared with laughter—all except for Cal, who only ever seemed to sneer. He shouted over the noise. 'Girl can't even spit out her own na—'

'Shut up,' Tyra snapped, without even glancing back at him (her attention was firmly on Danielle). She hoisted the backpack above her head, further out of reach. 'Say it. It's simple. Say, "Peter Piper picked a peck of pickled peppers".'

'Pl-please.' Danielle could not conceal the exasperation, the vulnerability in her voice. 'P-p-please, T-Ty—' She attempted to reach for her bag.

The dreadlocked girl swung it behind her back. 'No. It's puh-puh-puh *Peter*'.

Another chorus of enraging laughs ensued.

'Start again,' Tyra grunted.

Danielle stepped to the bully's side, making another feeble effort at reaching for it.

'*Whup!*' came the ripping thud as Tyra's free hand whipped around, connecting with the side of Danielle's head.

"Oooooh," the entire group jeered in unison.

Danielle made a delayed flinch and held a hand to her ear, which was now ringing, radiating heat.

'Nope,' Tyra said, wagging a finger. 'You didn't say it.'

The younger girl knew better than to take a stab at the phrase. She'd scarcely be able say it in an empty classroom with Miss Taylor; attempting it here was inconceivable.

'Pl-please…' She choked on air. 'I. I-I n-need. To. G-Go t-to…'

6

The baying hyenas cried in contentment and Danielle abandoned the sentence. Tyra merely stood there, unsmiling and impatient.

'Last chance, Stamyell…'

Danielle felt a burst of frustration. The banal nickname itself had never truly riled her; she was more affronted by its childishness—this person was practically a full-grown adult. 'T-Ty. T-T-Tyra…' she stuttered. 'I… I-I c-can't.'

'C'mon. You better. Or your bag is taking a trip to the roof.'

Danielle's eyes widened. 'No!'

She considered making a final swipe at the stolen possession but hesitated in fear of another clout.

'Then say it.'

Danielle took a breath, quickly weighing up her miserable options. Was there even any point?

Yes. She needed her bag.

She tried to block out the noise and disregard all the expectant eyes. C'mon, she thought, one word at a time…

'Peter…'

The group fell silent, an eager, expectant scorn present on each of their faces.

'P-P-Pipe. Pi-Pipe…'

All except Tyra erupted into interminable cackling. Deafening, penetrating beyond all measure.

'Too bad,' the bully said, emotionless. 'I gave you a shot.'

Like the recoiling of a trebuchet, Tyra lowered the backpack to the floor with an outstretched arm. Then she launched it with all the might granted by her gargantuan frame. Even Danielle couldn't deny that it was an impressive throw: the bag soared overhead, ascending four levels to disappear behind the filthy guttering of the social studies building—the only roof with no discernible access (which was doubtless no coincidence).

7

More hollers of derision ensued, and Danielle felt a sudden sinking in her chest as she bid farewell to all her stationery and workbooks.

Could there have ever been another outcome?

April 4, 1997

'Y-you don't th-think. M-My…sta-stammer is im-improving?'

'I didn't say that, Danielle. I just need you to be aware that the more comfortable you become talking with me the easier you might find it; I don't want you to confuse legitimate progress with a deepened level of rapport, or intimacy.'

'*Intimacy.*' Danielle snort-laughed at the word and screwed up her face.

Her teacher rolled her eyes. 'You do realise I've only given you this time because of how bright and *mature* I thought you were. Maybe I was wrong about the last part.' She shook her head but smiled, returning to Danielle's workbook to continue the pattern of descending ticks.

'I a-am g-grate…ful.'

'Well, good. I can't make this clear enough though: I'm not a speech therapist or coach. If you feel like the exercises we try aren't working, I'd suggest you ask to be referred to real specialist, O.K.?'

Danielle nodded, although not truly giving any credence to the notion. She adored Miss Taylor and their sessions; the opportunity to properly engage with the subject matter was entirely absent in any other setting. Here she could ask questions, demonstrate understanding, and pose her musings in her own unrushed time. While in regular lessons she was now utterly petrified of being asked for input.

Blinded by flawless grades—and apparently unmindful of her impediment—three of her Middle-school teachers had pushed Danielle to skip the final year and start high-school early. To them the decision seemed obvious; she'd learn nothing from staying. Unfortunately, no one had accounted for what a truly daunting experience the transition might be for the girl.

As is the case with most underfunded schools, Hopesprings High was not a forgiving place. Like predatory sharks, teenagers tend to have a knack for tracing blood in the water: peculiarities are often identified and swiftly attacked.

While it certainly didn't help that Danielle was a year younger than her peers, it was the stammer that they all fixated on; to the crueller kids it was almost exotic—a piece of bait far too enticing to ignore. After enduring several weeks of far from welcoming behaviour, she hadn't managed to read any of her book reports or essays aloud, and soon she was unable to answer a single question posed in classroom.

Fortunately, Danielle's chirpy English teacher had already taken a shine to her by this point, and remarkably, she'd volunteered to tutor her after lessons. While some educators genuinely care, Miss Taylor almost seemed to care too much; a woman for whom teaching was less of a vocation than a deep, spiritual calling (and who'd perhaps not even be embarrassed to admit to such a corny and trite-sounding thing in public).

While Danielle sometimes felt guilty for the added attention, in truth, she supposed that her new arrangement wasn't enviable; after all, few of her peers would be so grateful for *extra* schooling. And as her mom often told her: You must let the pendulum swing in your favour from time to time.

'Yes, perfect,' Miss Taylor said with a proud smile as she finished her marking. 'I mean, feel free to try more of the problems at home, but I think we can move on from integers and rational numbers.'

Danielle smiled and the teacher looked up at her clock.

'Wow, we've still got forty-five minutes left—you breezed through that even quicker than I'd anticipated.'

She leafed through her textbook for moment before hesitating and closing it.

'Hey, how about this. Are there ideas or topics you're interested in knowing more about, outside of the normal syllabus? Anything at all.'

Danielle thought for a moment.

'Um…H-H-How ab-bout d-de-terminism?'

The teacher stiffened up. 'Determinism. *Philosophy*… really?'

Danielle nodded. The word had come up twice in an article she'd recently read in Scientific American, but she only had a vague idea of what it meant.

'I don't know if I…' Miss Taylor leant back, pursing her lips, clearly battling with some kind of internal conflict.

Seconds later her posture relaxed though and she smiled. 'You know what, sure. Why not? Last week we talked about the *Many Worlds Interpretation*. So, what the heck.'

Danielle grinned, slightly relieved that her request was not seen as too impertinent or odd.

'I actually minored in philosophy at college, so I'm probably not the *worst* person in the world to ask about this. But, where did you even…' She chuckled. 'Never mind. This is like, twelfth grade stuff though—at the minimum.'

'O-O.K.,' Danielle said, still smiling.

Miss Taylor laughed again. 'All right. I will do my best not to butcher this…and forty-five minutes is actually no time at all to really delve in. *Determinism* is basically cause and effect, applied to all actions in the universe. It states that every event is the direct result of a previous event.'

'L-like… N-Newtonian mec-mechanics?'

'Um, in a lot of ways, yes. But determinism, as a philosophical idea, is basically the counterargument to us humans having freewill.'

10

'I-I see.' Danielle nodded.

'In fact, the determinist philosophy refutes the existence of freewill entirely.'

Danielle squinted as she tried to conceptualise this for a moment, already thinking a few steps ahead. 'S-So… We d-don't make… Our-our own ch-choices? E-Ev-rything is p-p-predetermined?'

'This is the idea.' The teacher leaned back. 'All right, let's try something…When I nod at you. I want you to immediately lift up a hand. It can either be left or right. But just pick one and do it.'

Danielle chuckled. There was five second or so pause before her teacher nodded. Danielle hesitated for perhaps a second, then swiftly raised her right hand.

'O.K., you raised your right. Now, someone arguing for freewill would say that it was your personal choice to pick your right hand over your left. But why? What was your rationale? Well, in a deterministic universe, you had no choice, the action was decided by forces out of your control—*unconquerable* neurological occurrences in your brain; a string of prearranged conditions.'

Danielle stared back inquisitively.

'A scientist called Benjamin Libet conducted a study not so long ago. He predicted, via brain monitoring electrodes, which small physical movements his participant would make, well before they admitted to consciously making the decision to do it.'

'S-So… I was aaall-always going to r-raise m-my right h-hand… I c-couldn't h-ha-have d-done otherwise?'

'Basically, yes. Again, advocates of freewill have tried to contend that there is *agent* causation as well as event causation: while most agree that the physical world is driven by cause and effect, the actions driven by us *free-thinking* agents are not. Hence, we can all have an effect on the universe by simply *willing* things to happen.'

Danielle smirked, immediately recognising the flaws in this argument. 'B-But y-you d-don't th-think that's… right?'

'Well, I don't want to say anything definitively. Consider it though, your mind is propelled by your brain, and brain states are still *physical* states. By that principle, your mind has to adhere to the same laws as the rest of the universe.'

'R-right…'

Danielle stared at the desk in front of her, squinting harder this time as she tried to process the implications; a few off-the-cuff sentences from her tutor had suddenly cemented swathes of comprehensive yet previously disparate information. Determinism suddenly made perfect sense.

For a thirteen-year-old, Danielle was well versed in Physics. On a fairly competent level she understood the causal nature of the universe: she knew roughly how particles functioned, how they're governed by physical law, and therefore the behaviour of all matter could conceivably be predicted via mathematical equations.

It seemed almost embarrassing to her then, that *this* philosophical penny had only just dropped; *all matter* followed a precise, predictable, and intransigent sequence, leading all the way back to Cause Number One: The Big Bang. *All matter.* Which meant her, her mother, Miss Taylor…every human that exists, *has* existed, and *will* exist on planet earth. People are no more able to decide their own actions than a match can decide not to combust when struck under perfect conditions. Freewill is not even an illusion—it's a fundamental impossibility.

The teacher watched Danielle for a moment with a look of mild concern. 'I know this might sound a little scary,' she said, softening her voice. 'I remember finding all this pretty disconcerting the first time I heard it—and I was a lot older than you. The idea that we don't have the kind of control we think we do…it's a hard pill to swallow.' She smiled. 'I don't want you to feel upset though, and this isn't the only idea out there. For instance, there's something called compat—'

'H-How d-d-does this fit i-in with The M-Many Wor-Worlds…'
Danielle interrupted, knowing she wouldn't need to complete her own
sentence.

Clearly tickled by this, and visibly relieved, the teacher let out a long
giggly laugh. 'Well…' she eventually started, 'plenty have argued that they
fit together quite well; in some ways it accounts for randomness. It's all
theoretical, but if there are an infinite number of alternate realities taking
place alongside our own, due to all the possible alternate actions, *these
universes* would still be equally deterministic.'

Danielle smiled. 'R-right.' she said. She'd been so enthralled by the
Many Worlds Interpretation since learning about it; it was pleasing to
confirm that the two ideas were compatible.

Miss Taylor suddenly adopted a lofty voice, awash with comic whimsy.

'So, in an alternate world, my fellow marionette, a minute ago you
lifted your left hand instead of your right…and for whatever reason, *this*
insignificant action, or countless others, could have sparked a whole chain
of alternate—yet equally pre-determined—events…a different life for you
entirely.'

'I-I l-like that…'

Danielle tried for a moment to picture a parallel reality identical to the
one she was currently living, save for a single variation, seemingly
insignificant…but enough to generate a complex sequence of altered
events.

May 12, 1997 (A.)

As she approached the dreaded busy hall in the English block, Danielle dedicated all her energy and focus on stopping her body from shaking. This was new: nerves so prevailing that they hinder basic movement.

Just get on with it… a little voice in her head asserted. She continued hastily down the corridor.

Seconds before reaching the classroom, however, she'd felt the sudden desire (or more of an inexplicable impulse) to **turn and look back at the way she'd come.** On doing so she immediately spotted the familiar and unsettling shape of tied up dreadlocks, floating in her direction like the prow of an invading Viking ship. The rest of the girl was blocked by the human traffic in front.

If Danielle had not looked back at that exact moment, Tyra might have seen her first—and the vicious eleventh grader had not once offered Danielle a free pass. Embarrassingly though, the sighting resulted in her nearly falling face first as she broke into a run; she tripped on an undone shoelace and was forced to steady herself on the door to Mr Herbert's classroom—thankfully without making too much noise.

She caught her breath and stepped inside.

The silence in the room was excruciating. She'd tried to gauge Mr Herbert's reactions at several intervals as he read her work, but his poker face was consummate. All she could do was wait.

A few minutes later the English teacher looked up, wearing a minute smile.

Surely that's good, she thought.

'Your understanding of the subject matter is evident, Danielle, exemplary in fact. You set out the ideas wonderfully and your perspectives are nuanced and expansive.'

14

He paused, placing down the essay. 'Honestly, these are probably some of the best arguments and counterarguments to the topic I've ever seen. I appreciate you taking the time. I only have one criticism…'

Mr Herbert ran his thumb and forefinger down the curved ends of his bristly moustache, then looked down as he slowly shook his head.

'But, I'm afraid it's a significant one. Well, it's everything, really.'

Danielle felt a tugging sensation in her stomach as she predicted what he was going to say.

The teacher sighed. 'I'm just afraid you won't be able to express any of this…off the page.'

She could feel herself becoming flustered. 'I. I-I know I…' She took a breath. 'I m-might not be-be…Be ready n-now. Bu-but Miss T-Tayylor is he-help-ing…me. A-And may-maybe in… s-si-six months…'

She took a longer pause and Mr Herbert waited, a sort of patient pity in his eyes.

'Or I-in a y-year—'

'I'm sorry, dear,' he interrupted. 'I can't let you to get your hopes up. You deserve my honesty: the debate team just isn't for you.'

He slid the hand-written paper halfway towards her across the desk, letting his hand linger on it for a moment.

'Your energy is best concentrated elsewhere.' He tapped the pages with his finger. 'Stick to writing.'

The teacher reclined in his chair. Something about the blasé way he did this irritated Danielle.

'You have a real talent,' he continued. 'But you'll never be able to match the conciseness, the succinctness you can achieve with the *written* word. I see big things for you. I do. You must be realistic though. Stay in your lane, set your sights on becoming an author perhaps. Or even a journalist.'

Danielle sunk her head and nodded.

Leaders speak though, she thought. Leaders don't win over a crowd with an essay or an article.

When Danielle left Mr Herbert (which she did in a relative hurry), her only friend in the school was emerging from a classroom two doors down.

Lea clocked her and smiled.

Danielle managed a small one back. 'De-Detention?'

'What else?' Lea said glumly. 'Why aren't you in the library?'

Danielle explained as they walked towards the front of the building.

In the heart of an impoverished inner-city in South Texas, the school was expansive but shabby. Even the newer sections were marred by broken windows and graffiti. A sad forecourt sported sparse patches of brown grass and a rusted flagpole with no flag. Lea was in the year above, which made her two years older (although the age difference appeared even greater than this). Aside from Miss Taylor, she was one of the few people Danielle could express herself to without being cut off or having her sentences finished for her. The younger girl also enjoyed how utterly different they were: Lea did not express any aptitude or fondness for academics, and self-consciousness was a trait she seemed to lack entirely. Perhaps this was why she was the only student comfortable associating with Danielle in public, while all the other avoided her like the plague.

The elder girl was not a popular student either. And the reasons were easy to identify: she swore like a sailor, belched often and unapologetically, and always spoke her mind, heedless of the repercussions. She wore her hair in a greasy ponytail, as well as the same pair of grubby looking dungarees day in day out, and sometimes her eyes were encrusted with smears of eyeliner she'd applied several days prior.

She basically did exactly as she pleased and cared nothing for the opinions of her peers—which seemed the worst transgressions a student could make.

They both lingered awkwardly by the entrance while Danielle waited for her lift home. A would-be latchkey kid, if her mother were not so overprotective, Danielle had to remain at school an hour or two each day before being collected. If she hadn't been with Mr Herbert today, she'd have likely remained in the library, studying well after last period.

'Look,' Lea said, 'I know you stayed up all night writing that paper, and I know it meant a lot to you, but it's just one dude's opinion. Fuck that guy.'

Danielle stared at her feet. 'May-Maybe h-he's r-right…'

'No way.' Lea said. 'You know those naysayers in every success story, the lame douches who tell the hero they haven't got what it takes? Mr Herbert is just one of those stupid, sucky, downer people, Dani. That's all.'

'L-Lea… d-do y-you… e-e-ever th-th-ink…'

Lea waited patiently, her head raised.

'…Ab-bout…al-alt-t-ternate re-al-lities?'

'Huh?'

'L-Like…ma-maybe th-there's a a…w-world where M-M-Mr Her-Herbert g-ga-gave me a sh-shot…at the deb-debate t-team?'

'Oh god. You're talking about that dumb film that just came out, aren't you?'

Danielle stared back blankly.

'Sliding Doors?' Lea tutted. 'I watched it with Tom. Oh my god, I didn't know a film could suck so hard for so long…If this is what you're talking about, then no, I don't believe in alternative worlds where all the best things happen to us, but we still fall down some stairs and die anyway…making the whole thing pointless. What a crock of shit.' She frowned.

'God, Dani, I thought you were meant to be smart—and original! And now I hear you ripping off dumb Hollywood movies?'

Danielle was so exasperated she felt herself shaking. She didn't know what to address first: that, especially in this context, alternate and *alternative* were two very different things? That the notion of parallel dimensions was very much postulated in theoretical physics and not just some banal Hollywood invention? Also, what reason did *Lea* have to discount such a theory?—because she didn't like a dumb movie?!

'You've got that look in your eye,' Lea said. 'When you think I've said something crazy or stupid and you're dying to rant at me…'

'F-F-F-Fir-First off…' Danielle raised her voice. 'The Ma-Many W-Wor—'

But the younger girl's impending diatribe was interrupted by the arrival of her mom in her battered old station wagon. She waved at Lea. Lea waved back before slapping Danielle on the shoulder. 'Chin up, Brainiac,' she said.

May 12, 1997 (B.)

Danielle approached the English classroom, essay in hand. It had taken her until three in the morning to finish and resulted in her struggling through the entire school day on two and half hours' sleep, but she'd done it.

She knew Miss Taylor would have argued her case well to Mr Herbert (after all, her mentor had arranged the meeting). Danielle was as satisfied with her work as she could have been, and he should at the very least be impressed by her producing five-thousand words on such short notice. All the pieces were in place; the only thing that remained was the stomach-turning task of convincing him.

Marching towards the door she soon became annoyed that her legs were trembling (a terrible look in such a busy corridor) and was forced to stop along the way. Here she experienced an unexplained urge to glance back at the hall behind her. It felt visceral, instinctual, like an animalistic wariness. ***A more rational impulse quickly emerged to conquer it, however, and she glanced at her feet instead.***

Damn, she thought—one of her shoelaces had become untied.

Annoyingly, the fastening knot had tightened rather stubbornly, and she took a moment to prize it undone, placing her essay beside her on the floor.

Just as she was retying the lace, she sensed someone approaching from behind. *Fast approaching.* Then she felt a hand on the back of her shoulder, followed by a forceful shove.

From her compromised position she toppled over, landing hard, sprawling out sideways on the floor. She looked up to see Cal's contemptuous face.

Tyra appeared soon after, with her small crew of sycophants already in hysterics.

'What you still doin' here, Stamyell?' the bully asked as Danielle struggled back to her feet. 'Don't tell me you've been in detention too?'

She looked down. 'And what's this?'

Both girls reached down for the essay simultaneously, but the larger one was victorious.

'*Religion* has a p-p-p-positive,' Tyra read with a mock stutter, provoking some more laughs, 'im-im-p-p-pact on the world'.

Danielle noticed the disdainful emphasis placed on the word religion.

'Wait, what?' Cal interjected. 'My brother is in pretty much all her classes—including social. No one gave *him* that assignment.'

Danielle twitched, staring at the assignment and praying for it to be returned.

'Oh really?' Tyra's mouth contorted into something resembling a smile. 'Well, if Cal says you didn't need to do it…' she slipped the essay out of its translucent protector.

'P-P-Please!'

'P-P-P-Please, what?' Tyra taunted. 'O.K., how about this. Say, "Red lorry, yellow lorry" three times and I'll give it back.'

Danielle hesitated for a moment, then decided not to take the bait. Meanwhile Tyra appeared to be silently reading the first page.

A moment later she looked up. 'You can't be writing arguments in favour of religion anyway, Stamyell,' she said. 'Religion is a disease.'

The bully paused contemplatively.

'I don't want people to think you're dumb, so I'm gonna help you…' She produced a lighter from her pocket.

Before Danielle could force out a note of objection, the corner of her paper had been lit. Within seconds the whole collection of pages was ablaze; the fierceness of the flames perhaps somewhat of a surprise to Tyra, who reactively withdrew her hand and left the paper to drift down to the floor, where it continued to smoulder. Lines and lines of fine compact calligraphy were reduced to ashen grey in a matter of seconds. Thick black smoke billowed towards the ceiling.

As she watched all her late-night efforts burn away, Danielle said nothing. She didn't see the point.

It might have been less painful though, she considered, if Tyra had held the flame to her skin instead.

'Hey, you there!' came a cry from somewhere behind them down the corridor.

'Run!' yelled Cal, and the whole group bolted, promptly chased down the hall by two faculty members, then a third considerably slower one.

Not wanting to answer any questions, or be forced to snitch, Danielle hurried away in the opposite direction, just as the third teacher was stamping on the glowing soot.

A little while later Danielle and her friend Lea were waiting outside the front entrance.

'Look,' Lea said. 'I know you stayed up late writing it, and I know—'

'I-I I... w-w-would ha-have s-sooner h-her l-lit m-my h-hair th-than that p--paper,' Danielle interrupted, maddened.

'Don't be so dramatic. Just explain what happened to Miss Taylor or Mr Herbert. I'm sure they'll give you another chance.'

Danielle frowned and vigorously shook her head.

'C'mon. The bitch committed arson in front of a corridor full of people. Anyone could've ratted on her...she won't know it's you.'

Danielle returned a distrustful look and the pair were interrupted by the arrival of Danielle's mom in her battered old station wagon. She waved at Lea and Lea waved back before slapping Danielle on the shoulder. 'Chin up, Brainiac,' she said.

As strong-willed as Danielle was, it'd been difficult to stop the events of the last few days from getting under her skin. As well as the disparaging words from Mr Herbert, she'd also had the misfortune of crossing paths with Tyra on several occasions. It occurred to her that remaining completely silent whenever she was faced with the towering tormenter might be the best course of action to take. Less ammunition, she decided.

Tyra had quickly cottoned on to this, however, and it seemed to merely incite more inventive methods of harassment.

Three days ago, Danielle opened her lunchbox in the cafeteria and found the girl standing over her.

'You don't mind if I have this, do you, Stamyell?'

Danielle pursed her lips like they were sewn shut.

'No? …O.K.' The bully delved into the box and pilfered her sandwich.

The following morning Tyra pushed ahead of her, blocking the door to the bathroom. 'Manners are everything, Stam,' she said. 'You gotta say "excuse me".'

Danielle turned with a sigh and carried on to her first lesson, where it took a decent amount of resolve for her not to wet herself. After a sprint to the bathroom that lunchtime, she waited in the queue, all the while eying a tray of blueberry muffins.

Tyra, Cal, and three other seniors approached her.

'Mind if we cut in?' Tyra said. 'No? …Thanks.'

Danielle suspected it was no coincidence that the five seniors took a muffin each, sneering at her before leaving the line.

By the time she reached the tray it was empty, aside from a few miserable crumbs, and she turned back to see Cal watching her.

He waved, dropped his muffin on the floor, and stamped on it before giving her the finger.

But the coupe de grâce happened yesterday, when Tyra blocked the corridor to science class, asking, 'What did we learn about "excuse me?"'

Danielle opened her mouth, quickly closed it again, then turned back on herself to race around the building and access the room from the other way. She arrived two minutes after the bell to a mild scolding from her teacher.

'This isn't like you, Danielle,' he said. 'Don't let it happen again.'

At least she hadn't given them the satisfaction of mocking her speech…

*

Lately Danielle was becoming especially irritated at having to wait for her mother at school, long after the final bell had rung; she'd sooner walk the streets than linger in this hellscape for longer than she needed to. Fortunately, Miss Taylor's sessions accounted for two of the five days; for the remaining three she elected to read under the huge oak tree at the top of the playing fields—her new shaded sanctuary.

Today, though, a downpour of rain had extinguished this possibility, and she desperately needed another Tyra-free zone.

While her friend Lea had invited her to a studying session (which was code for 'help me with my assignment'), she was presented with one more option: watching the school's first-string senior debate team face their inner-city rivals.

The obtuse and slightly smug Mr Herbert had given Danielle much to think about in their short exchange last week. Chiefly, why was he so adamant that she would never be up to the task?

Perhaps watching his team in action would shed some light.

Were they such sublime orators, imbued with talent that a speech-impaired wretch like Danielle could only marvel at?

As a Star Wars fan, she doubted this. She knew that James Earl Jones had shared her impediment, and the power and loquacity he'd managed to convey as Lord Vader taught her that miracles can clearly happen.

At lunch break, Danielle and Lea sat in the quietest corner of the cafeteria. The former was tensed up, rigid, and after furtively swallowing a spoonful of her tomato soup, she'd peer over her friend's shoulder.

'Why the fuck do you…' Lea said, briefly turning around. 'What's up?'

'N-Nothing,' Danielle replied. 'Ju-Just b-been a r-rough week.'

'God, don't tell me you're still stewing over the—Hey, what the hell d'you keep looking at?'

Danielle sighed. 'T-Ty-ra's been re-relent-less la-laate-ly.' She gave a long pause. '…I-I I've h-had t-to t-ta-take a v-vow of siii-lence.'

'A vow of silence?' Lea raised an eyebrow. '*Oh*…Less ammunition?'

Danielle nodded.

'And how's that working out for you?'

'N-Not gr-great…'

Neither of them said anything for a moment, then Lea decided to change the subject. 'You still up for studying with me in the library later?'

Danielle paid her a sceptical look. 'Wh-Whaat a-assign-ment d-d'you n-need h-help with t-today?'

At first her friend feigned incredulity. Then she huffed. 'English…'

'A-Actually, I th-thought I-I'd ch-check out the deb-debate team.' Danielle replied. 'It's the f-f-finals.'

'Gonna see what all the hype is about?'

Danielle shrugged.

'Well, they'd better be absolutely shit-hot if they've turned you down. Screw English. I'll come with.'

The large assembly hall was less than modestly filled, as she suspected it might be; these kinds of proceedings could never garner the same devotion seen at any of the sports events. Not wanting to draw any more of this finite and precious attention away, the pair surreptitiously found their seats halfway along a vacant row and awaited the show. Mr Herbert was on the stage, apparently hosting.

'Good evening, everyone,' he bellowed into the microphone from his podium. 'Welcome to the 1997 DHSA national Debate Finals. Hopesprings versus Westmeadow'. The moustachioed teacher cleared his throat. 'Both of our teams have been prepped and are raring to go, so I'll simply go about introducing the topic of the evening.

'I must say, it's a relatively controversial one, but we hope our teams can remain *Christian* about it—mind the pun.' He grinned obnoxiously as the small audience remained silent.

Danielle cringed, considering that some teachers should probably never attempt humour, no matter how innocuous.

'…Sorry, you'll all get that in a moment.'

Danielle rolled her eyes.

'The statement our teams will be debating is: Religion has a positive impact on the world'.

A frown crept across Danielle's brow. Couldn't he have thought of a different statement for *me* to discuss in my paper? she thought.

She paid Lea a look.

'What?' Lea mouthed.

'The affirmative team will be represented by Westmeadow, while the negative team are represented by our hosts, my very own Hopesprings High. I will now let each speaker introduce themselves.'

The first was a scrawny, spotty faced senior in a lurid floral shirt. He looked altogether terrified to be there.

'Hello, m-my name is Quentin Stevens, and I'll be representing the negative team.'

He was the typical breed of student associated with these events: a student afflicted with bad acne, worse teeth, and an equally unfortunate haircut.

From his introduction, Danielle did not think he gave the impression of a charismatic interlocutor. And as she continued to listen, she discovered that neither did his female counterpart (whose address could barely be heard, even with the microphone).

Lea's expression professed the same sentiment; they both frowned as the other three students feebly introduced themselves and their standpoint.

Several minutes later the rival Westmeadow student was stumbling through a long and laboured opening statement.

'…Where, for example, would we be without the Golden Rule? "Do unto others as you would have done to yourself". Respected scholars maintain that this—not to mention a plethora of other religious doctrine—is the very foundation of our moral code…'

Danielle made a face, disliking both the statement and its poor delivery. Reasonable arguments, she permitted, but nothing with any weight behind it.

She soon found herself becoming distracted, her mind hastily wandering in the directions she'd have steered *her own* opening statement, only zoning back in when the speaker was making his conclusions. Then she politely clapped along with the forty or fifty people sitting in the vicinity.

It was always a disadvantage to speak first, Danielle knew. Although both teams are equipped with well-devised openers to regurgitate at will, those going second had the option of also attacking their opponent's one, and thus the opportunity to gain more points from the judges.

'Ah, I remember you saying it's not helpful to start first,' Lea whispered. 'The other team can immediately diss your premise.'

Danielle nodded and smiled somewhat proudly, but then put a finger to her lips.

'Sorry,' Lea hissed back.

Low murmurs of conversation arose from the audience during the break, and Mr Herbert made a silencing gesture. 'And now for the opening statement of the negative team.'

Everyone focused on the first speaker, Quentin, who for some reason looked taken off guard. He breathed heavily into his microphone.

'Uh, g-good evening, Ladies and Gentlemen,' he mumbled, with his head down and hand visibly shaking. 'I'm afraid I…must begin by immediately disagreeing with my opponent.'

Danielle nodded encouragingly. Better, she thought.

Quentin stared at his notes for longer than was acceptable and appeared to silently mouth the words. He mopped his brow with the trembling hand.

'I, um. Well…I definitely do not share the view that religion is the basis of morality. Almost without question it can be attested that altruism is a deeply primeval attribute, not a religious one. Our species would never have been so successful without it…' His words were rushed but audible.

'Erm, there was mention made of the Golden Rule: "do unto others as you would have done to yourself". This, I do not believe, is something that has ever needed to be taught. I would argue that it is such an intrinsic value, one might even call it the basis of empathy itself, which we all know is an emotional state so instinctual, so entrenched in our psyche, that it surely predates any religious teachings.'

The longer the student on stage spoke, the lower Danielle's bottom jaw started to fall; her mouth was now fully agape. She'd written it, the speech Quentin was unsteadily uttering. It was practically verbatim—and any paraphrasing he employed simply dulled its potency.

Lea looked at her, perplexed. 'What?' she whispered.

'Th-Those a-are…M-My words,' Danielle said loudly, drawing some attention.

'Huh?'

'…As we continue to grow as a society, we generally become more open, and our values become more progressive and inclusive. This natural evolution of our moral code, however, is entirely at odds with the ideals espoused by any religion…which seemingly tend to grow more outdated by the day.'

Quentin took another prolonged look at his notes.

Danielle pointed at him and let out another harsh whisper: 'He's r-reading f-fr-from m-myy e-essay!'

'No way.'

'It would stand to reason that those claiming the higher ground should be the authority to follow. But in reality, it is *they* who are playing catch up…'

Danielle shuffled in her chair and mouthed the words almost in unison with Quentin, occasionally shaking her head and biting her bottom lip.

'Wait. Is he reading from the essay Mr Herbert assigned you last week?' Lea mumbled.

Danielle nodded, still outwardly seething.

'No. He can't do that!'

Was this some form of conspiracy? Danielle thought. Had Mr Herbert searched the school, deceiving handfuls of students, prising them of their input and then barring their entry onto his lineup? Was the teacher aware of such great chasms in his team's reasoning, and his desire to win *so great*, that he had to resort to such blatant plagiarism?

As the debate continued, certain answers were given. As far as Danielle could tell, no other student's voices had been stolen; all of the rhetoric spoken was hers and hers alone.

28

She could only bear so much, and after the third round of applause directed at *her* late-night turmoil she stood up, staring at Mr Herbert for several seconds in enraged disbelief.

At the end of their recent meeting, she'd watched him with some confusion as he placed her essay in his desk drawer. Embittered though, freshly wounded by the rejection, she didn't even ask why he'd kept it— besides, what use was the paper to her at this point anyway?

Danielle suddenly felt a fierce desire to confront the man, to scream at the top of her lungs and demand an admission of guilt, an apology, an explanation at the very least…

She knew though that even with all the bravery in the world, and without any fear of reprisals, it would never play out this way. Her indignation, her outrage, all of her inwardly eloquent fury would be reduced to a splutter, a pathetic whimper, distorted and essentially unexpressed.

Lea stood up with her, taking her by the arm. 'C'mon. Let's go.'

May 19, 1997 (B.)

It had been a strangely tranquil week following the flaming essay incident. The injustice of the experience was almost balanced out by Tyra's subsequent suspension—a reprimand the bully had thankfully attributed to the teacher who'd caught her in the act, instead of Danielle.

Miss Taylor had spoken with Mr Herbert and explained the situation. He offered the student another two days to rewrite, which she managed in one. The trusted mentor had considered, however, that their designs on her joining the debate team were perhaps premature, suspecting that the debate chair had already made his mind up regarding Danielle's suitability (and may have simply been humouring her). For the time being then, they'd decided to focus solely on her speech therapy; any prospects of debating could wait till the start of the next academic year—dependent on how well she'd progressed.

In an attempt to accelerate this, Danielle had been researching vocal exercises and other methods in the school library (as well as she could in any case, with the limited literature available). She'd wanted to delve deeper into this today, but presently her friend Lea's studies had taken precedent.

The pair were sitting in the furthest corner of the library, with the younger student checking over a sloppily handwritten essay.

'S-Say r-r-regardless or…I-I-Irrespective. N-Not "irregardless",' Danielle said as she pointed at her friend's paper. 'A-And i-it's "f-for aaall i-intents and p-p-purposes", not "all i-intensive p-purposes".'

'Oh. Thanks,' Lea mumbled, blushing slightly. Then she looked up. 'Hey, you sound like you're hesitating a little less when you speak. Are those sessions working better now?'

Danielle started to nod, but it morphed into more of an uncertain shrug; she didn't know if they were. Either way, it wasn't happening fast enough.

30

'Um, I know Tyra ruined that essay, but what's happening now? …Like, with trying out for the debate team and all that?'

Danielle released a small sigh. 'M-Mi-Miss T-T-Taylor and I…w-we d-decided i-i-it m-might b-beb-better to p-p-post-p-pone.'

'I guess… if she thinks'—Lea stopped and screwed her face up—'wait, why were you writing essays for Mr Herbert anyway? He's not even your teacher.'

Danielle paid her friend a look of incredulity. 'S-so h-he c-caan s-see h-how well I can r-rea-reason…'

'Reasoning on paper isn't really the issue though, is it? You have zero problems there'. Lea paused, seemingly unsure of whether to verbalise what she was thinking. 'I did actually see something a couple days ago…something that I thought might interest you.'

'What?'

'So… On sixty-fifth and third, a few doors down from that gross bagel place we went to that time, I saw a sign outside a bar. They do like an open mic night every month…for Spoken Word Poetry'.

Danielle recoiled, staring open-mouthed at her friend.

'Hear me out. I know how you like writing poems, and I just thought that maybe—not now—but in a couple months, if your speech is improving, you could maybe write something and perform it there?'

Given no response whatsoever, Lea continued.

'…I think you have to be sixteen to enter, but they're hardly gonna ask for ID if you're not drinking. Anyway, a touch of mascara, and you'd pass for sixteen.'

Has she lost her mind? Danielle thought; she couldn't imagine anything more terrifying.

Lea was watching her expression and laughed. 'Well it might be something worth trying? …You'd get out of your comfort zone, build up some experience in public speaking.'

'L-Lea…' Danielle started. 'J-Ju-ust. No…'

'*Dani*,' Lea said, playfully mirroring her. 'Just promise me you'll think about it. I mean, the debate team is competing in the hall now. Don't you want to be on the stage with them one day?'

Danielle was well aware that the debate team were in session. Since her attempt to join them had been delayed for several months, however, any desire she felt to watch them had waned.

'F-fine,' she said, only to appease her friend.

She'll forget all about it in a day or two anyway…

Lea waved goodbye to Danielle at the gates and embraced her new boyfriend Tom, a lanky senior with a crew-cut. He was garbed in exclusively green clothing and an American flag backpack. Immediately, the two started passionately making out. Danielle grimaced, watching them for a moment with mild disgust before heading in the opposite direction.

She walked to the far corner of the High School perimeter, all the way to the very rear of the sports field where there stood a wooden fence with several panels missing. After side-stepping through the largest gap, she picked her way through a sorry assortment of trees and bushes and emerged in a run-down residential area.

While all the areas directly bordering Hopesprings High were ugly, and shabby, and dilapidated, this particular region had the added element of danger.

The student tightly gripped the straps of her abnormally heavy rucksack as she navigated though the slum-like suburb, pretending it was jetpack capable of propelling her to safety.

She knew the block well (as did the local News Station), and this instilled the unnerving sense that something traumatic could occur at any given moment.

The longer she walked, the more she felt like she'd entered a kind of wild, chaotic dimension where the usual rules did not apply: the few shops she passed were gun and liquor stores; children younger than her were coordinating unconcealed illegal exchanges on the corners; two homeless men fought over what looked like a pink stiletto shoe.

Fortunately, she did not have to venture much further. She headed straight towards a grey apartment block with several boarded-up windows, the highest rooftops of her school still visible behind her. An old man with a greying afro and an unkempt beard was sitting on a deckchair outside the block reading a newspaper. He acknowledged Danielle as she approached and muttered something inaudible. As the entrance to the building was propped open, she hurried inside and immediately ascended the stairs.

On the second level, the floor was strewn with broken bottles and junk food wrappers. A soiled sleeping bag rested in a crumpled position in the far corner; she suppressed a small shudder and breathed through her mouth as she knocked on the door of apartment 21B.

After a nervous ninety seconds, Sonya answered the door, holding her baby in one arm. Her stern, apprehensive expression softened when she registered Danielle.

'Oh hey, sweetie,' she said. 'Come on through.'

Danielle wiped her feet, from habit only, and followed her inside.

'Amber-Lynn!' Sonya yelled down the hall. 'Aunt Dani is here to see you.'

As always, Danielle chuckled at the peculiarity of the designation. She and Sonya were cousins—which would make her the little girl's second cousin. She enjoyed this mildly authoritative title, however, and voiced no objections.

Although Sonya was young, perhaps not even twenty, she did not appear so. With eyes blemished by surrounding dark circles and faint resting lines and an unnatural greyness to her complexion. She'd lost several of her teeth already, and the remaining front ones were starting to discolour and corrode. The evident cause of this was upsetting for Danielle to reflect on, and so too was remembering that she'd once considered the relative pretty.

Inside, the apartment was akin to a crack den—almost farcically so. Her rooms presented no signs of renovation in the last few decades. The carpet was worn to practically nothing and springs were protruding from a stained beige sofa in the corner of the living room.

Amber-Lynn was sitting on the floor watching cartoons, barely more than a foot away from a small TV with a crooked antenna, the front of which apparently held together with masking tape.

'Look! Here she is,' Sonya said in an overly animated voice.

Danielle smiled at the little girl. She turned and smiled back but soon became bashful, running over to cower behind Sonya's legs.

Sonya laughed. 'Why you gone all shy for now?' She tutted and turned to Danielle. 'She's been askin' after you all week.'

'Aww, i-it's O.K.,' Danielle said. She crouched down slightly. 'I h-have some-something f-for you…'

Danielle heaved her bag off her back and dropped it on the floor with a thud, massaging her shoulders and the strap-shaped groves left behind. She leant over and unzipped the bag to produce a doll, a few years old but in perfect condition. Then she dropped to her knees, holding it out to the infant with a smile.

The little girl leant forward and her eyes widened.

'Oh wow, look at that,' Sonya said. 'What do you say to aunt Dani?'

With slight reluctance Amber-Lynn moved out from her mother's legs and accepted the doll from Danielle.

She looked up shyly and grinned. 'Fanks.'

Danielle chuckled and started removing the rest of the objects from the backpack. She produced several packets of pasta and ramen noodles, and perhaps a dozen canned items, utterly relieved she'd no longer need to lug it all around.

'Thi-This i-is all I c-could g-get f-for now…but I c-can br-bring m-more iin a f-few d-dayyys.'

'No, you're an angel', Sonya said, eying up the spoils. 'You sure your ma's O.K. with this?'

Danielle nodded—not at all convincingly—before changing the subject. 'H-Have have y-you h-heard any m-more…A-About m-moving in wi-with au-aunt B-Bea?'

'Nope, still waitin'. I know *she's* cool with it. It's just her feller needs convincin''

'D-do y-you thi-think sh-sh-she will? …Con-Convince him?'

'Who knows? I been tellin' her I'd pay my way. If I moved in there, I could go back to waitressin' while she watches these two lil monsters.'

Sonya walked towards the sofa and gently placed the baby (now fast asleep) down on the middle cushion. She covered him with a blanket.

'I think Bea likes the idea. She always wanted kids. Him though, not so much.'

Her voice suddenly cracked and wavered. 'All's I know is, I gotta get out of here, Dani. It's never been safe. And it sure as hell aint gettin' better.'

Danielle nodded gravely, understanding everything and nothing about statement. She didn't want to know details; she just wanted to hear when things did, in fact, get better.

The Casio on her wrist suddenly caught her eye.

'Oh no…S-S-Sonya, I'm s-orry. I, I've got t-to go ba-back.'

'Already? But you just got here.'

'I'm s-sorry. I didn't re-realise the t-t-ti-ime…I s-said I'd s-see m-my tutor b-before m-mom p-piiicks me up'.

She hurried out of the building, back towards school. Again the man in the chair muttered something in her direction. It unsettled her, but she knew better than to engage. She could feel his eyes burning into the back of her head as she rushed away.

Danielle was certain something was a little off from the moment she'd entered Miss Taylor's Classroom. The teacher seemed on edge, ushering Danielle into her seat in a brusque manner, intermittently clicking her pen, withholding her typical air of warmth and cordiality.

'So, I couldn't help but read the essay, Danielle.' She sighed. 'It was beautifully written, as I'd expected…'

'Th-Thank—'

'But that's not what I wanted to talk to you about.'

'I-It's n-not?'

'No. This is difficult for me to tell you. I take it you didn't watch the debate in hall this afternoon?'

Danielle shook her head.

'O.K., so, I think'—she corrected herself—'I'm pretty *certain* Mr Herbert thought he was the only teacher who'd read your work. Because he…' She paused. 'Well. He stole it, Danielle.'

Danielle squinted. 'H-He st-stole it?'

'He got one of his debaters to use your essay in the finals. Every single word of it.'

'What? Wh-Why?'

'I guess he was impressed by your arguments. I know he really wanted his team to win…and thanks to you, they did.'

'B-But…th-that's ch-cheating.'

'It was original writing, so he knew the judges would just assume Quentin—the team captain—had come up with it all himself.'

'I-It's p-pl-plagiarism.'

Miss Taylor gave a slow nod. 'I know.' She took a breath and lowered her voice. 'O.K., I'll level with you…Mr Herbert isn't exactly a popular figure among us teachers. Let's just say he steps on a lot of toes. But…I know how much you want a place on that team so—'

'N-Not anymore.'

'Excuse me?'

'I-If h-he did that…I…I-I don't wa-want t-to be…o-on hi-his t-team anymore.'

The teacher bowed her head slightly. 'I understand. What would you like me to do next? I can report him to the principle? And Quentin too, for going along with it. Although I guess his behaviour is…' she trailed off.

Danielle thought on this for a moment. Now that the shock had almost faded the situation just seemed rather pathetic, to the point of being almost amusing.

'No,' she said finally, with a faint smile. 'No… just l-let th-them both h-have i-it.'

What an utterly moronic move this was.

Danielle thought back to the initial conversation and wondered why on earth she'd told Lea that she'd even consider it. That brief window of equivocation had been enough to incite months of relentless harassment. It'd been nearly six since her friend first mentioned the idea in the cafeteria, and Danielle had barely gone a day without hearing about it. The recurring questions: 'Are you ready yet?' followed by, 'C'mon, wouldn't you rather just get it over with?' and finally, 'Surely now is the time?'

Lea just wouldn't let it go.

If something was ostensibly in Danielle's best interests, it seemed there were only so many times she could think of an excuse not to do it before she was forced to lay down her shield in surrender. Now that the time had come though, it scarcely felt like it *was* in her best interests. It felt like an act of social suicide; an entirely unconquerable mountain which she now stood at the base of, untrained and ill-equipped.

Danielle had let her hair grow out over the summer, and on Lea's instructions she was wearing make-up for the first time in her life. Neither change, however, had made her feel like she had any business being where she was. She continued to peel and scratch at the label of her lemonade bottle, wondering if her heart would ever resume its normal tempo. Various aspects of her setting only functioned to intensify her anxiety: the low-lighting, the smell of cigarettes and alcohol, the worn-out woodwork enveloping every corner—the very idea that she was unaccompanied in a bar to begin with.

There were several speakers due to go up before her, and still plenty of time to back out. She'd somewhat painted herself into a corner though. Where could she go? Her mom wasn't going pick her up until 10pm…Besides, it'd taken a week to convince the woman to let her attend, and then another week to stop her from assisting on chaperoning; was all this effort to be wasted?

You've practised it a thousand times, Danielle said to herself, remembering that last hundred were seamless.

She controlled her breathing, trying to block out the noise from the steadily filling bar; it was becoming livelier, noticeably louder.

She closed her eyes, thinking, If you can recite your work in an empty room with no one listening…just imagine you're back in that empty room when you get on stage.

This notion emboldened her to a degree, due to its logic. But right when she felt some confidence creeping in, so did another thought:

Stay in your lane.

Nearly a full year had passed since the vile teacher had said it to her. Some phrases just stuck.

She hopped down from her stool and walked over to the compere. He was jotting something down with one hand and swigging a large amber coloured beer with the other. He smiled when she approached.

'I-I…' she started

"Sup, sweetheart?'

'I'm. S-Sorry. I-I just. C-Can't do this,' she sputtered. 'C-Can you cr-cross m-me…o-off. The l-list?'

He studied her for a moment. Then he gave a small nod. 'Yeah…To be honest, when you came and signed up, I *did* wonder. No problem. I'll cross you off.'

While the man's reaction wounded her, it was nothing compared her own sense of self-loathing when she skulked, head down, back to her seat; the elimination of anxiety and restored feeling of calmness were of no consolation whatsoever.

Slumped over her table, she watched the remaining speakers. Some were enlightening, others not. One caught her attention more than the rest: a huge man with a patchy beard and a voice that seemed to rumble like thunder. This criminal-turned-professor recited a poem about his struggles with prejudice in the academic world.

He belted out the last line in his booming baritone: 'With my voice, not my fists.'

The speaker replaced the microphone and a weighty ovation poured from the fifty or so people in the bar. Two men even stood up and whistled. Danielle clapped along and continued to watch him for a while after he'd taken his seat. Eventually he noticed, locked eyes with her, and smiled. A fatherly kind of smile. She felt a strange and powerful urge to approach him.

And do what exactly? she thought. Struggle to spit out something unintelligible and expect him to just stand there and wait?

In any case, it was nearly ten o'clock by this point; she knew she'd better check the front for her mom.

Hunched over the bar table, Danielle continued to peel and scratch at the label of her lemonade bottle.

From the moment she'd had the 'no alcohol' imprint stamped on the back of her hand, her heartrate had remained at its elevated pace.

'…Light faces; dark intent. Big cars; small minds. Weak excuses; strong conviction. "This is not your world", they say. With their eyes, not their lips. "I'll change your mind", I say. With my voice. Not my fists.'

The huge patchy-bearded speaker gave a slow nod before reuniting the microphone with its stand. A weighty ovation poured from the forty or so people in the bar. Two men even stood up and whistled. Danielle clapped along, praising the universe that she didn't have to follow him.

She'd sat through five performances so far, and while no one else had been as captivating as this criminal-turned-professor, voicing his struggles with prejudice in the academic world, they all shared common ground: none had fluffed or fumbled their lines.

His delivery in particular was flawless; while Danielle *had* liked the words, she sensed he could've read out the label of his beer bottle with similarly enthralling effect.

She'd committed the ordering to memory. There was only one other participant to speak before her now.

Suppose this person just fell apart… she thought. Or if they were to say something bigoted or bizarre? Something obscene or shocking? It could be anything, any kind of faux pas to lose them the crowd and incite an unfavourable response; this might well take some of the heat off her.

Danielle tutted to herself. In truth she wouldn't wish such things on her worst enemy.

If the next person on stage *had* committed some huge social blunder, the girl probably wouldn't have noticed anyhow. Despite her best efforts, her leg had not stopped trembling and the sweat was now practically pooling in her palms.

The older woman currently on stage was performing something of a monologue of her life experiences. It wasn't particularly poetic, from what Danielle could tell, but it was well received by the audience and the woman seemed admirably confident—unflappable even. Part of Danielle willed her to carry on. Have all night, she thought.

This was scared Danielle though.

Suck it up… brave, self-improvement Danielle responded. You've practised a thousand times in your bedroom, she reminded herself. You've recited it with no mistakes, no stammers, and no hesitancies. You can do this.

The older woman started to wrap things up.

'…So, I said if I ever marry again, it'll be for money.'

The audience laughed and applauded generously. Danielle became breathless as she joined in with them, unsure if her legs would even carry her to the stage.

Thirty seconds later the compere was calling her name, and her heart was exploding in her chest.

Oh God, oh God, oh God…

She jumped inelegantly from her stool and hurried towards the microphone stand, keeping her eyes fixed on the battered floorboards, profoundly conscious of the beads of perspiration forming on her brow.

Her head remained down as she stepped onto the platform.

'H-Hello…' She exhaled into the too-high positioned mic, producing a minor whistle of feedback. 'This is, "A r-river. N-Not a w-well."'

Bad start, she thought.

'A f-f-force un-unto it-self.'

Long pause. Though a part of her was surprised she'd even blurted out the first four words under these conditions.

She scanned her audience, which was a truly dreadful idea. The perplexed looks she noticed were beyond hindering.

'La-Lann-Language.' Huge gulp of air. 'Me-Me-an-Meanders…'

Deathly silence.

'C'mon, girl. Move it along!' someone yelled.

Several fierce shushes were directed at the individual. Everyone else seemed genuinely annoyed and the heckler was pacified. But this was the final death knell for Danielle. She knew there'd be no returning from here.

She looked up for a moment and locked eyes with the large professor, who was sitting no more than a few feet away.

'Take your time, sweetheart,' he said with softness.

The horse, however, had long since bolted. Any ambition of trying to claw the performance back was an exercise in self-deception.

Nevertheless, she took a breath, attempted to calm herself, eventually opened her mouth to start again. Nothing came out.

Then she felt the first inevitable tear slide down her face and decided she had to move. Off the stage. Away from all the eyes. Anywhere but here.

Several feet to her right she spotted someone with long blonde hair slowly exiting the bathroom; ignoring the gentle protests of her audience, she sprinted for the door. After ducking under the blonde's arm and hurrying inside, she sought refuge in the first cubicle she found and bolted it shut. Only now did her sobbing draw sound: heavy gasps and snorts driven by hyperventilation.

Hysterics were far from Danielle's nature though, and it only took a minute or so to pull herself together; as soon as she'd achieved this, there was only one thing she wanted to do. She knew full well that she could perform the piece in its entirety without any mistakes—but she had to prove it to herself once more. Already it seemed infinitely easier in here, her four-panelled sanctuary, her impenetrable stronghold, far removed from a cruel and callous world—it barely mattered that it was in fact a grimy cubicle in a filthy public bathroom.

'A River, not a Well,' she said faultlessly, closed her eyes, and began.

'A force unto itself, language meanders free and unencumbered. The fierce enemy is stunned, its soldiers suddenly feeling outnumbered.

'No sooner able to *fade* than to *freeze* in an instant. No sooner able to *halt* than to become non-existent.

'Expressions arise and prose flows, where the sentence is going, hell, the writer barely knows.

'Positions assemble and concepts take shape, forming the basis of a persuasive landscape…

She smiled (that part had been the trickiest), then paused and took a breath.

'But what use are armies when they cannot engage? …What use are words when they're confined to a page?

'Each proud assertion, although well researched, remains silent, unheard; *bald eagles*, merely perched.

'So the words must be spoken, announced to the masses. Declared to one's peers and her teachers in classes…

'The moment draws near, for the great river to veer, out to the ocean of aired ideas.

'But *what's this in the way?* A cheap trick has been played: an obstruction, a dam, a colossal blockade.

'Try as it might, the water travels no farther. The shields of the enemy block the arrows of the archer.

'Remove this embankment and allow my words to run free! Why gift a vault of insight and offer no key?

'I'm a ballerina bound to a chair just yearning to dance. I have both vision and flair; please give me the chance.'

She gave a final breathy pause before continuing.

'Until then I'm plagued with this terrible affliction. Incapable of clarity and completely robbed of diction.

'"Become a speech writer", they say. "Lend your words to other voices." As if this were a lifeline; a heroine of choices.

'But I'd sooner stay a river, and fight the dam in vain, than be a well for others, to siphon off and drain.'

She remained seated, let out a small sigh, and resumed her dismal sobbing.

But a few seconds later she's interrupted by distinct, unusual sound. The echoing thuds of a person clapping.

'Exquisite,' came a voice from the other side.

Somewhat disturbingly, she noticed it was a man's voice. And a deep one at that.

'I do have a couple questions,' the man bellowed.

'Um…' Danielle started, 'th-this i-is th-the gi-girls b-b-bathroom…'

'Ah, so that answers my first question: did you know you'd entered the men's room? *No*, I take it, is the answer to that.'

She took a sharp inhale. Oh no…

'Don't worry, dear. Happens all the time…The last time *I* made that mistake was after one too many cocktails at a beach bar in Maui. Though, I imagine being faced with my three-hundred-pound self was probably a fair bit more startling for those poor gals.'

Danielle let out a short involuntary chuckle, realising who was talking to her.

'Y-You're th-the pr-pr-professor?'

'I am indeed.'

'H-ow…How. Mu-much d-did…You h-hear?'

'All of it…I was about to interrupt you after the first line—and I'm delighted that I didn't.'

Danielle remained silent.

'Now, I don't know about you, dear. But I'd quite like to continue this conversation. Though I don't think this is really the appropriate place. Do you?'

'Uh. N-No,' Danielle agreed, despite feeling a strong reluctance to leave her sanctuary (even after discovering that it was a disgusting *boy's* sanctuary).

'O.K., well how about this: I'll help smuggle you out unnoticed and we'll go find a quiet place in the bar to talk?'

'Um…' Danielle deliberated aloud. While the idea of heading anywhere with an enormous stranger seemed unwise, he'd made no suggestion leaving the bar. In fact, he was offering to *rescue* her from the men's room. 'A-A-All-right.'

'Great. Hang tight. I'll tell you when it's safe to come out.'

A few seconds later Danielle heard the exit door swing open, then the sound of another man's voice.

'Oh, sorry, sir.' Danielle heard the professor say. 'The owner is just fixing a very minor plumbing issue. Do you mind coming back in five minutes?'

'Oh. Um, yeah, sure,' came the response.

Danielle smiled to herself, realising it'd be difficult for anyone to argue with the huge man.

'Right,' the professor whispered. 'You can come out now.'

After wiping her face with the sleeve of her sweater, Danielle obliged.

When she stepped out, she saw the giant holding the door ajar (though entirely blocking the open space). He looked down at her and smiled.

'O.K., step behind me and stay close.'

She quickly realised the professor's plan was fool proof; he was so large that as Danielle tracked side-on between him and the wall, she was completely concealed. Although this hardly seemed to matter anymore, as everyone was now focused on a new speaker on stage. It was as if her moment of mortification had never happened.

'How about over there?' he muttered covertly, pointing towards a secluded table.

Danielle nodded.

At either side of the table was a large armchair and small low stool. She decided it'd be impractical for her new acquaintance to take the latter, so she settled on this and waited as he ambled by her, lowering himself into the chair with a faint groan.

'Well, it's nice to speak with you without a toilet door between us. My name is Jarrell.' He held out a hand for her to shake. It felt like she'd barely managed to grip his top two or three fingers as she did so.

'D-D-Dan…nielle,' she said. 'I… l-liked…Y-Your po-em.'

'Well, thank you very much. I thought *yours* was exceptional. It's a shame no one else got to hear it.'

Danielle gave a simple nod.

'*But* I did notice one mistake: you said, 'the water can travel no *farther*', to rhyme it with archer. Spoken in proper English, farther should only be used for physical distances—you use 'further' for figurative ones.'

Danielle saw his point and took slight umbrage with it. 'B-Bu-Buut. Wh-What about. Po…etic. Li-licence?'

Jarrell grinned. 'Hmm. I suppose I can give you that. And, it *is* a sweet rhyme. Be a shame to cut it.' He regarded her for a moment and raised an eyebrow. 'Say, how old are you?'

'F-Fourteen.'

'*My Lord…*' Jarrell leant back and exhaled. 'Trying what you did would have been difficult for *anyone* your age. Attempting it with a stammer…well, *damn*…'

Danielle felt a warm prickliness roll across her face.

'I'm sorry. Don't be embarrassed. When I was your age, I had a rather pronounced lisp. Damn thing infuriated me. Didn't shake it until I was seventeen.'

'R-really?'

'*Oh yeah*. Though let me tell you, in most circumstances, a lisp is far easier to shed than a serious case of alalia syllabaries.'

47

Danielle showed her confusion with a raised eyebrow as she held his gaze for the first time.

He smirked. 'You see, this is somewhat of a specialist subject for me. I'm the professor of language at the community college down the street. *Speech therapy*, though...that's my true passion.'

Danielle felt a curious buzz of excitement, a wave of static along the hairs on the back of her neck. What a chance meeting this was.

'That poem. It gave me the impression that you've got some pretty serious aspirations. What do you want to be when you're older?'

Danielle was unsure how to respond and considered downplaying her answer.

Screw it, she thought. The man was a stranger; what harm could it do to be honest?

'The f-f-firrst e-elected fe-female p-p-president of the U-United S-S-States.'

Jarrell nodded. 'Ah, but you're so young—what if another gal beats you to it?'

'Th-then,' she said, unfazed, 'I-I'll b-be. S-Second. Or...th-third.'

'Well...' Jarrell's expression betrayed zero emotion. 'If that's your goal. You're going to need some coaching.'

A smile crept across Danielle's face. This was the first time anyone had ever responded to her lofty dream with any kind of seriousness. Just to be humoured was a minute shock; which was why it took a moment to process what he'd said.

Could he really help her?

She realised she was getting ahead of herself. 'I... I-I d-don't...' she started glumly. 'H-H-Have... M-Mon-ney f-for that. M-my...M-M-Mom...D-D-Doesn't—'

'I don't need your mom's money,' Jarrell said with shortness. 'I would simply need her permission. First though, tell me…to date, which president has had the most positive impact on the American education system?'

Easy, Danielle thought. 'Ei-s-s-sen-sen…Eisen-hower.'

Jarrell seemed to contemplate her answer. Then he smirked, seemingly in approval.

'In your opinion, what was the most important court ruling, amendment, or policy implementation of the twentieth century, in terms of its bearing on education? —make your response as *brief* as humanly possible.'

Danielle was thankful for the caveat. She also appreciated the dry humour in it.

'B-B-Brown v-ver-sus B-Board. N-N-Nineteen f-f-fifty…four,' she said, with as little hesitation as she could manage.

A grin materialised on the professor's face, the largest one so far, and they stared at one another for a few seconds in silence.

Danielle's eyes narrowed; she prompted him with an inquisitive tilt of her head.

'Well, if I'm to be responsible for coaching a future president,' Jarrell explained. 'They had better have their priorities straight.'

At lunch Danielle and Lea were sitting at their usual spot in the quietest corner of the canteen. Lea had just returned with a large plate of spaghetti, and Danielle stared at the packed lunch untouched in front of her.

'So, how come you didn't you call me?' Lea said, listlessly dissecting a rather unattractive meatball.

'S-Sorry i-it w-was late…I—'

'It's O.K.,' Lea dropped her fork and grinned excitedly. 'Just tell me how it went. I've seriously been frickin' dying to hear.'

'Oh…It w-was…I…I d-don't…'

For a moment the older girl carefully studied Danielle (who forcibly avoided her gaze). Then with a look of sad recognition, she said: 'You didn't go up, did you?'

'I h-had e-ev-ry in-in-inten-tion. I-it's j-just—'

Lea's eyes flashed with further dissatisfaction. 'You didn't even try?'

'L-look. I-I I w-wennt,' Danielle started, flustered, having not anticipated such a solemn reaction from her friend. 'Th-That's… A-All. W-We ag-agreed o-on.'

'No, Dani. I don't think that *is* what we agreed on.'

Danielle looked down at the table as her friend attempted to make deliberate eye contact.

'*I* thought the agreement was that you'd try.' Lea's voice started to break. 'You were meant to write something, rehearse it over and over again in your room, until you—'

'I d-d-did. I-I—'

'Do you know what I see in you?' Lea interrupted. 'Do you know what everyone with half a brain can see?'

Danielle remained silent.

'We see someone so intelligent, so brilliant, so capable of great things…and they're throwing it all away.'

'Lea, c-c'mon…'

'No.' Lea raised her voice. '*You* c'mon. I understand it's hard for you. And I can't imagine what it's like to have all those amazing thoughts swirling around in your head and not being able to express them. But you have to try. And you have to start now, or I can promise you you'll wake up one day full of regret. Because it'll be too late.'

'Lea, I-I'm s-sorry. L-look, I j-ju-just can't—'

'No. Save it. I'm done pushing you. I'm done trying to get you to do stuff you *clearly* don't want to do.' Lea stood up and reached down for her backpack.

'Hey.' Danielle stood up with her. 'L-Lea.'

'You infuriate the shit outta me. Do you realise that I wish I was a *fraction* as gifted as you are? That I wish I didn't have to struggle through every stupid class? That I had the *tiniest* inkling of what I'd be able to do when I leave this place? But you, you know exactly what you want to do. You know where you want to go, all the steps you need to take to get there. And you're wasting it all.'

They sat in awkward, intolerable silence for a moment.

Then when Lea spoke again she was quieter, her tone colder.

'What you have is a serious wound, Danielle. And the way I see it, you have two options: you can either treat it, and eventually it'll heal and go away. Or you can let it fester, like you are doing, and one day the damage will be irreversible.'

With that, her friend turned and marched away, leaving her still steaming plate of food on the table.

Danielle felt a heady dose of guilt and resentment, mingled with a searching kind of shame. It echoed the feeling that her friend had truly hit a nerve; there was veracity to her outburst.

But how dare anyone try and frame it so simply? Danielle thought. Like there was some easy fix, like she was *choosing* to stay on the course she was on.

She spent the next two lessons stewing, replaying what Lea had said to her over and over. After the final bell she drifted down the corridor to her session with Miss Taylor. The first half an hour or so flew by far too quickly and Danielle recognised that she'd barely engaged. She only became present when her mentor's demeanour seemed to shift.

'No, Danielle. You need to hold your breath for seven.'

'Oh…s-sorry…'

'Let's try again.'

'O-O.K.'

'Right, long exhale. Pause. And say "how now, brown cow"—remember, emphasis on the vowels.'

'H-Howw…n-n-noww. B-B-Broww'—Danielle stopped and shook her head—'S-Sorry…I…'

She was still far too distracted to concentrate.

'Danielle.' Miss Taylor said, rubbing her temple. 'I feel like we may have reached the point of diminishing returns.' She sighed. 'There's only so far I can take you. I think it's time you start looking for someone more experienced. Someone qualified, you know?'

'I-I I'm s-s-sorry Mmm-iss Tay-Taylor, I'm. Just. A li-little d-distracted.'

'Oh, sweetie. You don't need to apologise. These past few months, I just think we've started to plateau, and all I want is for you to improve'.

'I…I-I th-think…I-It's. S-Still. H-Helping,' Danielle said, not at all honestly.

She was comfortable with Miss Taylor; she didn't want to look for anyone else. The very mention of it terrified her.

'As for me tutoring you on your other subjects. Well, I really don't see how much help that is anymore. I feel the only thing that's going to accelerate your learning is moving you up another grade, which I'm sure you'd handle with ease. On paper, at least.'

The teacher let out another sigh, a powerful one this time. 'The bad news is that I think they're unlikely to do this if your speech doesn't improve.'

'It w-will.'

Miss Taylor appeared to recoil slightly in her chair. Then she looked away. 'O.K., Danielle, there's something else I have to tell you. This isn't going to be easy, so I'll just come out and say it.' She paused. 'I'm moving to Chicago.'

Danielle shook her head. She tried to speak but the shock of the statement stole her initial attempts. 'Wh-When?' she eventually managed.

'In a couple of months…My partner's been offered a job there. We had to take it. I'm sorry, Danielle.'

The girl lowered her head.

'But this might even be a good thing for you.'

'A g-good th-thing? …H-H-ow?'

'Treat it as an opportunity to find some else to help you with your speech. If you're going to beat this thing, you need a professional to coach you, someone with real knowledge.'

Beat this thing? Suddenly the impairment seemed to take on an even more sinister form; as if she were battling some desperate terminal disease.

'B-Bu-But… I-I. D-Don't w-aant… A-Aany-one else.'

For the first time ever, Danielle left Miss Taylor's classroom far more deflated than she'd entered it.

She seemed able to acknowledge certain pivotal moments in her short life; whether their significance was legitimate and somehow ordained, or if she was simply the one ascribing meaning to them, was unclear. As she walked down the corridor on the verge of tears, however, she considered that this timely blow was the antithesis of an opportunity.

Although occasionally the closing of one door meant the opening of another, this particular juncture seemed nothing other than a dead end. There were no other doors in sight.

She couldn't expect her mother to fund a private speech therapist, especially with no guarantee that it'd even work. She'd never had to contemplate such a dramatic deviation in her life's trajectory before. Was it really possible…that her dreams were, in fact, unreachable?

Her friend was right; some people were born with certain gifts. She was lucky enough to be gifted with intellect and a thirst for knowledge, which she could likely apply to a number of avenues. She had to face the facts though: public speaking was almost certainly not one of them.

Danielle and Lea were sitting across from each other in the quietest corner of the canteen for lunch, the former happily munching on a sandwich, while her friend had just returned with a large plate of spaghetti and meatballs.

'So, how come you didn't you call me?'

'Y-Yeah. Ab-About that...' Danielle was almost giddy with excitement. 'I I-I ended up st-st-staying l-late. T-Too l-laa-late for c-calls, m-mom said.'

Lea smiled, but then flashed her a puzzled look. 'Why would you end up staying any later?' She raised her voice. 'Hey! You still need to tell me how it went.'

'Oh, s-s-orry...I-It went te-terribly...' Danielle said, totally deadpan. 'I ch-choked.'

'Oh no, seriously?' Lea pouted. 'You got up and tried though, that's the main...' she trailed off before raising an eyebrow. 'Wait, then why the hell are you so happy?'

'L-Let's j-ju-just say...I m-met some-one. S-S-Someone p-pretty sp-spe-cial.'

Danielle smiled widely, oblivious to how her comment might be interpreted.

Lea laughed. 'I see! Well, it's about time really.' Her eyes narrowed. 'Hold on. You were in a bar...How old are they?'

'Um, I I d-don't know. *Old*...l-l-like...f-forties or f-f-fifties?'

Lea suddenly looked horrified. A meatball rolled off her fork and onto her plate, splashing sauce everywhere.

The pair continued to fumble around the misunderstanding for a further ten minutes or so. It wasn't until her friend mentioned the word 'grooming' and threatened to tell someone that Danielle understood the confusion and quickly explained herself. Lea's resultant laughter was loud enough to stop several conversations nearby.

Later that evening Danielle was slowly examining the professor's quaint and humble office. A resounding air of assurance arose from looking at the diplomas on the wall. She felt in thoroughly safe hands.

'O.K., listen up while I rattle off some information and go over the ground rules,' Jarrell said with authority. 'First off, *you are not* one of my students. You call me Jarrell, and only Jarrell. I'm off the clock, so this is simply one friend helping another friend, y'understand?"

Danielle nodded, eager to thank him but hesitant to interrupt.

'And one day the younger friend will become president and arrange some badass tax breaks for college professors.'

Danielle laughed.

'Good, *laughter*—you'll soon learn that this an integral part of the process.'

The professor briefly explained his schooling (which still sounded impressive despite his attempts to downplay it).

'…I've been a certified speech-language pathologist for the largest chunk of my career. And I've been helping people with severe disfluency issues for over a decade. If I had to guess, I'd say around eighty-percent of those people shared your exact problem.'

Danielle nodded again. Her confidence was growing.

'Now, I'll tell you what I've inferred so far. For starters, by gender alone, you are a rare case. Stammers are four times more common in boys than they are in girls.'

She was unsure if this was a good or a bad thing.

'I'll explain why this is in your favour,' Jarrell said, as if anticipating the query. 'Five percent of children are affected, and only one percent carry it through to adulthood. Fortunately, the improvement rate for girls is also considerably higher than it is for boys, and the retrogression rate is lower. Meaning, once they're on the path, they're more likely to stay on it.' He paused with the hint of a smile. 'So, congratulations, on your first great achievement…'

Danielle raised an eyebrow. 'M-My firrr—'

'Well done for being born female!'

The professor let out a booming chuckle, and Danielle couldn't help but laugh along. The man's joyful demeanour was infectious; he seemed to irradiate positivity.

'Now, many would argue that there is no *complete* cure out there for the chronic stammerer.'

Danielle felt a twinge of disappointment; though she'd never said it outright, Miss Taylor had often alluded to this.

'I, however, would argue that those people lack spirit and imagination.'

The girl grinned, then felt guilty for unconsciously attributing such negativity to her beloved tutor.

'Now, I'd go ahead and bet all my worldly possessions that your stammer is developmental, not acquired. You've had it for as long as you can remember?'

Danielle nodded.

'*Yeah*…in which case, it would've been more advantageous for you to have met me a few years ago. The earlier the better, really.'

She looked down.

'But you're still an adolescent, so we're catching the tail-end of the wave. And we're gonna pop up and ride that wave for all it's worth, O.K.?'

Danielle smiled, nodding with vigour this time.

'I'm also going to assume that you've tried to get help before?'

'Y-Yeah.'

57

'How old were you, the first time you did that?'

'E-le-leven.'

'Before that, I'm guessing your mom thought you were just going to grow out of it?'

'Y-Yeah.'

'It's not as crazy as it sounds. A lot of kids actually *do* just grow out of it. So we can cut her some slack there.' Jarrell smiled. 'In terms of your treatment, have you seen a registered SLP before? Or am I the first?'

'Um, I th-think y-you're the first. I w-work with M-M-Miss T-Taylor. B-But sh-she's n-ot cert-certified.'

'O.K. then. I'm gonna go out on a limb here…while I'm certain Miss Taylor is an angel, with no professional background, it's also very possible that she's been doing more harm than good.'

Danielle leaned back, again feeling another pang of guilt for her trusted mentor.

'Now, stammering is a very personal disorder, and it's often situational. In many cases it depends how self-conscious the individual is. For some, this isn't the most prevalent factor. But for *you,* I believe it's the primary one.'

Danielle and her tutor had never discussed this. Though mindful that her self-consciousness might be a reason, they mostly thought of her condition as genetic—the other variables were regarded as minor complications, unfortunate stressors, rather than a definitive cause.

'I witnessed your varying disfluency first-hand when I heard you in that bathroom stall,' Jarrellcontinued. 'You thought no one was listening, and you barely stammered at all.'

Danielle felt silly for not considering such a thing sooner. It now seemed so rational, so blindingly obvious.

'O.K., onto my methods. I am personally against medications and electronic speech fluency devices. I tend to favour fluency shaping therapy, role playing, and perhaps my most eyebrow raising approach: mantra meditation.'

This was the exact reaction the two words provoked in Danielle.

The professor smiled with confidence. 'Yeah, we'll see how you feel about it when our two hours are up.' He clapped his meaty hands together. 'Right then, let's get down to it. We know you can speak well when you're alone. I want you to highlight an example of a social situation where your speech fluency is best, and a situation where it is worst. Best one first, please.'

'W-Wi-With, Mi-Mi-Miss T-Taylor, my tutor.'

'Fair enough. And your worst?'

Danielle frowned. 'Wi-With T-Tyra.'

'Who's Tyra?'

'J-Just a girl f-from sc-sc-school.'

'I see…'

The professor went about introducing different hypothetical scenarios and having Danielle act out accordingly. It was difficult and awkward at first, but he was exceptional at putting her at ease. After a few practises it almost felt natural, as if she were actually interacting with the people themselves.

An hour and ten minutes into the session, Danielle became dumbfounded by the effectiveness of the mantra meditation. She was given strange Sanskrit terms to repeat, coupled with precise breathing instructions. What initially felt absurd and nonsensical, soon became relaxing and strangely empowering. The spiritual elements were no longer kooky, or cringe-inducing. Astoundingly, they started working.

'Empty your mind, rid it of clutter, and focus only on the mantra,' Jarrell said in a soothing voice. 'When you find yourself distracted by other thoughts, don't worry, simply refocus your attention and bring it back to the word: "*Gaur-Ra-Ang-Ga*".'

'*Gauranga*,' Danielle repeated with perfect fluency.

It was miraculous—her previous self-consciousness had all but evaporated.

With only fifteen minutes left of the session, Danielle was flooded by that recurring guilty feeling, the sense of disloyalty to Miss Taylor. The facts were undeniable: an hour and forty-five minutes with the professor had trumped hundreds of hours' worth of coaching with her.

'These sessions are also about engaging in conversations,' Jarrell said, affecting a different tone. 'Effective discourse is a deep part of the process. Let's talk about some topics you're interested in. Anything at all.'

'O.K.,' said Danielle, feeling a rush of strange déja vu. 'D-Determinism.'

Jarrell smiled but remained silent for an uncomfortable amount of time.

Just as she thought she'd made a mistake in presenting this particular subject, the professor dove into it with a level of understanding and nuance she had no idea he'd be capable of (after all, even some of the greatest minds favoured the illusion of freewill).

Though Danielle made the odd interjection, she was far more interested in what Jarrell had to say.

'…I'm no philosopher or neuroscientist. I like to *think* we're free to make choices. To carve our own destiny. I like to think I freely made the choice to step away from crime, that I *chose* to re-educate myself.

'Determinists would easily counter that this blueprint was already laid out, though—by my past experiences, my environment, by society itself. And I might argue, if that were the case, would I not be compelled to continue the more conventional cycle? To stay in the projects, keep pushing drugs? As far as I can tell, no factors, intrinsic or extrinsic steered me into teaching.'

'But…' Jarrell smirked. 'I think this is the point: it must have always been in my blueprint to break the cycle. *Feeling* like we're free is not the same as *being* free.'

Danielle wore a wide smile, nodding for her new friend to continue.

'I think that fortune favours the bold. And if we really are these damned puppets of biology, like a lot of very smart people believe, then be thankful you're a *bold* puppet—not one who merely goes through the motions feeling sorry for themself, for the cards they've been dealt and the way their strings are being pulled. *Act* like you have purpose, I say. Even if it is an illusion.'

June 8, 1998 (A.)

The condominium Danielle and her mother lived in was situated within a tight row of dishevelled low-income housing. When a friend once enquired about the style of the buildings, her mom had joked that the overarching theme of their street was 'damaged and discoloured'. Some of the other condos featured a boarded-up window or two; although all of theirs were presently intact, the building had definitely seen better days.

Danielle's tiny bedroom was slightly shabby and threadbare but otherwise orderly. A poster above her bed depicted a family of cartoon chimpanzees; one baby chimp was sitting in the corner, isolated from the others, and the lower-third displayed a well-known quote:

> *"Better to remain silent and be thought a fool, than to speak and remove all doubt."*

Presently the girl was lying in bed with her eyes wide open (a state she'd been in for most of the night). She heard a knock on her door and immediately let out a sigh.

'You all right, sweetie? You're usually up by now.'

With great effort Danielle rose. She then skulked downstairs, fixed herself a bowl of cereal in the kitchenette, and joined her mother at the breakfast bar.

'You know, the silent act is getting pretty old now,' her mother said, peering over her newspaper.

The girl continued to eat her breakfast without acknowledging the comment.

'It's been three months. I know you miss your old teacher, but it doesn't mean you have to give up.' She dropped her paper, trying to force eye contact now.

'I'm sorry we can't afford to find a professional, I really am…but why does that have to mean that you stop trying? This isn't the daughter I've raised.'

Danielle responded with a limp shrug.

'Don't you still want to get into politics when you're older?'

This comment was the first to land as intended. Danielle winced but still said nothing.

'O.K., fine. If you're in more of a listening mood, then listen to this.' Her mother made firm eye contact. 'I can't afford to keep replacing the food in the cupboards, d'you hear me?'

Although Danielle's heartrate picked up, the expression she returned was one of innocence and misunderstanding.

'You know exactly what I'm talking about. And no more after-school excursions. From now on you're to wait inside the building until five thirty. Don't think I won't phone in and check.'

Three months without any kind of speech coaching had seemed to erase every pen stroke of progress Danielle and her former tutor had developed in their private lessons. Little by little Danielle had embraced the idea of becoming a mute—romanticised it even. She considered that there was a mysterious kind of charm to the experience. When you didn't speak, fewer people could pepper you with their preconceptions.

Her views of Determinism also seemed to allay any guilt she might feel in not reaching her potential: if she failed to ever improve her speech and lived out a whole life with a stammer, she was destined to do so. If she pursued a career in the written word instead of the spoken, she was destined to do so. If she became a journalist, not a politician, she was destined to do so. This was simply fate as the universe devised it. She was not the wind propelling the wave towards the shore; she was the wave, *and* the shore, and momentum could only run its course.

While at times it did occur to her that this view was more fatalistic than deterministic, freedom was absent either way.

The route from Science to Math class was a typically treacherous one of late. She knew Tyra could emerge from any corner at any moment. Now that the bully was in her last days of school, Danielle took solace in knowing that these encounters were finite and fleeting. Unfortunately, though, this likely made them more treasurable to Tyra. And the senior was certainly not going to abandon any final opportunities of torturing her favourite target.

As if Danielle's thoughts were capable of summoning demons, the familiar, terror-inducing voice suddenly echoed along the corridor from somewhere behind her.

'Stamyell!'

Act like you didn't hear her, Danielle thought, picking up her pace.

'Hey c'mon now, I know you're dumb, but you aint deaf,' the senior yelled, catching up with her.

She bounded in front and completely cut her off. 'Listen. I need you to help me with something.'

Help her? Was she serious?

'So, you know I'm nearly done here—sad news, right?' Tyra paused for a reaction and Danielle gave her none. 'Anyway, my assignments have all kind of crept up on me…'

Impossible, Danielle thought. But still she gave no response.

'Well, I'm going to need you to write them for me. So I can focus on other stuff.'

This seemed a desperate move. In the catalogue of past abuse, the girl had never asked Danielle to do her work for her (which was actually somewhat surprising, all things considered).

'Now, this might seem like a lot to ask. We can forget about it if it is; I don't want to be unreasonable. So, if you don't want to do it, just say…'

Danielle opened her mouth. Mute or not, she could surely muster some form of objection to this obscene request.

'Just say, "She sells seashells by the seashore,"' Tyra said, grinning.

'T-Ty… Ty-ra.'

The name was the first word she'd uttered in weeks.

'No. That's not what I said at all. One more time. C'mon, at least try the first part.'

'T-Tyra…' Danielle panted in frustration. 'P-Pleea…'

Tyra shook her head and sighed. 'Fine then,' she said, pulling a photocopied page from her bag and handing it forcibly to Danielle. 'The first one is trig. I'll need it done by the end of the week.'

*

After her first lessons of the day, Danielle decided there was no point in delaying the inevitable. She bypassed the cafeteria, skipping lunch to get to work on Tyra's trigonometry assignment. With fifteen minutes to spare, she'd completed something of around a B+ standard (a marked improvement for the senior, she presumed, but perhaps not enough to arouse suspicion).

Danielle supposed that Tyra would at least be satisfied to receive the paper so far ahead of the requested deadline, which comforted her when she spotted the bully in the corridor. She pulled out the assignment in anticipation.

The girl was alone, listening to her Walkman and throwing textbooks into her locker. She noticed Danielle from her periphery just as she was turning away, slid one earphone to the side, and looked down with a blank expression. Danielle held out the paper.

'What's this?' the bully muttered, frowning.

Danielle nodded towards the paper in her outstretched hand.

Tyra glanced at it. 'Oh,' she said, rolling her eyes. 'I wasn't being serious about that, Stamyell. Jesus, you're such a tool.'

She tutted and walked away, leaving Danielle still holding the paper.

'Now, this might seem like a lot to ask,' Tyra said. 'We can forget about it if it is; I don't want to be unreasonable. So, if you don't want to do it, just say…' The bully paused with a grin. 'Just say, "She sells seashells by the seashore".'

This was a pivotal moment, Danielle thought. The truest acid test. All the free-flowing sentences achieved so effortlessly in a room with Jarrell meant nothing if she couldn't speak under these strained conditions. She attempted to calm the turmoil in her head, to block out the distractions and pretend she was alone in the corridor. Then she took a breath and made the verbal leap.

'She sells. Seashells. By *the seashore.*'

It was slow and ponderous, with an upward inflection on each of the last three words, but she'd said it without making a mistake.

Tyra stood there gawking at her for a moment.

Danielle smiled back at her abuser, conveying all the stillness and assurance of a snow-covered mountain peak. 'That's what you wanted me to say, isn't it, Tyra?'

Yes! a voice cheered inside her own head; this next sentence had felt almost as effortless as breathing.

She waited eagerly for the dreadlocked demon to respond.

But Tyra was impassive for a moment, simply staring back at her without saying anything.

It was entirely unclear what reaction might follow. Anger? —perhaps a violent outburst? Or would she continue posing verbal challenges until one of them reached their desired, stutter-inducing effect?

Neither of these things happened. In fact, if she didn't know any better, Danielle might've thought she'd noticed the corners of Tyra's mouth twitch, curling upward for a fraction of a millisecond. It was far too quick to process, however.

Eventually the senior broke her silence. 'Yes,' she said, almost solemnly, 'that's what I wanted. Guess you're off the hook.' The bell rang and the bully turned to walk away.

In many ways it was pure luck; Danielle was certain she'd been about to buckle. She could sense the warning signs: the breathlessness, the brief flutter of chest palpitations. Tyra couldn't detect any of this though. Those two short sentences, as far as the bully could tell, were a demonstration that her favourite punching bag was suddenly heavier and far more resistant.

*

Danielle strolled towards Sonya's building after school, still riding high from her encounter with Tyra.

Just like last time, the man with the greying afro was sitting outside on a deckchair. He was wearing a stained white vest today, smoking a hand-rolled cigarette while he read his newspaper. As Danielle approached the stairwell, he muttered something in her direction, his words much clearer than they'd been previously.

'If you lookin' for the girl…she gone.'

Danielle turned around, confused at first. Then she thought of something and her eyes lit up. She walked back out of the building and faced the man, emboldened to reply.

'She m-moved in with h-her aunt?'

The man didn't bother to look up from his paper.

'No. *Gone*. Dead…O.D.'d last week.' He uttered the statement as casually as telling the time.

Danielle gasped like she'd been kicked in the stomach. This was exactly how it felt: a forceful strike, delivered without warning.

'N-No. Sh-Sh-She wouldn't. She wou-wouldn't do that. *Her kids*…She loved them.'

67

'Seems she loved the pipe more.'

The tears started to form in Danielle's eyes, but the shock prevented them from coming completely.

'Are...are th-they O.K.?'

The man finally looked up at her.

'Mhm. CPS took 'em—they seemed fine.' Something briefly flickered across his blank stare; it resembled compassion, or pity. 'Least they both outta here,' he said, exhaling a plume of smoke.

Within a heap of trash on the floor, a patch of bright red fabric caught Danielle's eye. She disturbed the pile with her foot and out slid her old doll, the one she'd given to Amber-Lynn. Its eyes now seemed knowing, somehow full of sombreness and regret.

*

Later that evening she and Jarrell were partway through their session. The news had sunk in now, and Danielle felt crushed by it. While she and her cousin had never been that close—and her visits were at most a monthly thing—she felt like the only relative who hadn't given up on the woman; Sonya's own side of the family had cut ties long ago (including Danielle's mother). This meant that there was essentially no one to grieve with, no one who'd respond to the news with anything other than: 'Silly girl' or 'Could've seen that coming...'

She was slightly slumped forward on her chair, a far-off look in her eyes.

'O.K., Danielle, before we continue, you're gonna need to tell me what the hell it is you're wrestling with. You look like you could break down at any moment.'

'Oh...' Danielle said, still miles away. 'I-I I'm s-sorry. I...' It crossed her mind to invent another story, something less significant, but she sensed he'd see through it.

'I went to visit m-my c-cousin today. A-And I f-found out that…th-they died la-last week.'

Jarrell's voice softened. 'Damn…I'm sorry to hear that. She must have been young?'

Danielle nodded. 'A-And It's j-just. Sh-she was…Sonya…she was ju-just so selfish.'

'Selfish? How so?'

'She…she die-died f-from a drug overdose…a-aand she ha-had two ch-children.'

'I see. And you think this makes her selfish because she should've put her children first? No addiction should be stronger than her love for them?'

Danielle nodded.

'Perhaps that's right…tell me, where did your cousin live?'

'Cl-Clements Way.

'Ah. I know it well—awful place. And was she a single parent?'

'Yeah.'

Jarrell paused, he leant back in his chair and ran his hand over the bristles on his face. 'You know, Danielle. During the 70's, in Canada, there was a series of studies into drug addiction, using rats…'

At this Danielle looked up for the first time, completely nonplussed.

'Each rat lived in a tiny cage with two dispensers. One containing water, one morphine. Once they tried the opiate, they couldn't control themselves and started abusing it. Choosing it over the water. Over life.'

'O-O.K.…'

'In the same study, another set of rats were housed in a colony. An equal proportion of males and females. The colony was two-hundred times the size of one of the cages used—ample room for mating—with balls and wheels for play…Oh, and the same two dispensers'

Danielle sat upright, still sombre but no longer distant.

69

'Now, *these* rats almost exclusively chose the water; they rejected the morphine. And the ones who continued taking it took much smaller doses.'

He let out a breathy sigh.

'I used to know a lot of addicts, Danielle. All from around the same hellhole I grew up in. And I can tell you, their bad decisions all boiled down to an unwise—although perhaps justifiable—form of escapism. Just like with the rats in that experiment, if their choices were as simple as a fulfilled life, or an endless supply of drugs, none of them would have chosen the latter.' He paused for a moment. 'Besides, dear, I know how you feel about freely made choices…'

June 16, 1998 (A.)

It was a deeply curious thing. But Danielle supposed so too was the mind of any bully. In the week or so following Tyra's Trigonometry assignment demand (and her casually playing it off as insincerity later that day), she'd taken to ignoring Danielle in the hallways. Danielle first assumed that the senior simply hadn't seen her, or else was biding her time—like the cat who toys with the mouse before devouring it. On the third or fourth occasion, however, the pair locked eyes. The younger girl had readied herself for an onslaught: whatever heinous method of torment the bully had patiently devised.

No such attack came; Tyra merely flashed her a vague and imperceptible look. Although Danielle couldn't pinpoint its significance, if pressed, she'd say it was look of disappointment. This, as well as being downright strange, was fairly infuriating. It inspired an uncomfortable feeling she was unable to place. As the senior walked away, a strange urge had overcome Danielle. An impulse to shout after her: *What the hell is your problem?*

Though, of course, she said nothing.

In any case, she supposed she should have been thankful that Tyra had finally lost interest, and equally thrilled that in a week their paths would no longer cross. Good riddance…

Danielle waited at the usual spot in the library for Lea, who'd briefly mentioned meeting her after final period. Unsurprisingly, their bond had become strained in recent months; as any friendship might suffer when one half limits their dialogue to monosyllabic responses, hand gestures, fast scribbles on a notepad. For the first time, however, there'd been a shortness to the way Lea had addressed her at lunch. She seemed colder, coarser.

Glancing at the clock, Danielle noticed her friend was ten minutes late. When twenty minutes passed it became clear she wasn't coming.

Four new PCs with an internet connection had been added to the rear section of the library. Danelle had played with them a few times since their installation. Most interesting to her were the recommended online forums she'd come across: message boards where she could connect with other students from around the globe (an observation she still found remarkable) to discuss journalism and politics. Here, in this virtual world, she could communicate freely, without the boundaries or obstructions experienced in real-world exchanges. Her typing did all the talking for her. A career in writing would also offer this kind of freedom, she supposed. And the prospect gave her optimism.

As she contributed to a President Clinton inspired 'thread', as it was called, she realised this means of interaction could easily become another world to lose herself in. And why not? she thought.

Although writing may always be a consolation prize for her true ambitions, perhaps it was better to stay in this new-found lane. She should surely be thankful to have found another lane at all.

June 16, 1998 (B.)

Ever since Tyra had been rebuffed by Danielle's flawless execution of *She sells seashells*, there had arisen a bizarre energy between the two of them. The younger student had been primed to face further battles; prepared to tackle more difficult phrases on demand, even welcoming it as a form of training. 'This is it,' she'd mutter to herself when she spotted the group of seniors heading her way, controlling her breath as she did in her sessions with Jarrell. It was almost exciting.

The challenges never materialised, however. Instead, Tyra let her pass through the halls unmolested, occasionally paying her the odd glance but more often walking by with little recognition. On one strange instance, the senior made eye contact and nodded. Danielle was sure she was supposed to return a nod of her own, but instead she froze and stared back blankly.

But today, as Danielle made for the library, she heard that familiar whistle. Shrill and piercing, the noise had provoked reflexive fear in her for the best part of three years. When Danielle turned, Tyra was only a few feet away.

'What changed?' she asked abruptly.

'Excuse me?' Danielle said (happily without hesitation).

'You know,' the senior asserted. 'What happened to start you talking?'

Danielle felt acutely unsettled. Why was this terrifying person suddenly addressing her like an equal, talking to her so casually? Was it a trick?

'Um. I've been having speech th-therapy,' Danielle said, rattled by her slight fumbling of the final word.

Here it comes… she thought, bracing herself for abuse.

'Oh,' Tyra said, sounding almost dissatisfied with the answer. 'Well, it seems like it's working good.'

'Um. Yeah,' Danielle replied, too bewildered to think of any substantial response and wondering what the hell was happening.

Just as she was starting to think the conversation couldn't become anymore surreal, the senior remarked: 'You know, I had a stutter once.'

What? No. This was definitely something Danielle did not know.

'You…You did?'

'Yeah. Until I was about ten or eleven. I didn't go to therapy though.'

'Oh. Oh really? Um…how. H-How did you lose it then?'

'Hard to know,' Tyra said. 'My stepdad would probably take credit. "She's weak," he'd say to my mom,' Tyra looked up somewhat in a daze, as if recalling something difficult. 'Weirdly religious guy, he was. Used to say that my stutter was the devil speaking through me. He said God cursed my tongue because I was a sinner—liked to push shit like that on me when I was small.'

Danielle considered this for moment. It was hard to picture Tyra as ever being small.

'…Said he had to beat it out of me. Gave me difficult things to say back to him. Tongue twisters, you know? Stuff like that.'

Yes, Danielle thought, nodding. *This* she knew all too well.

'Yeah, well, some days I'd do all right. Some days I wouldn't. On the good days I got a nod, and he'd leave me alone. Little mistakes maybe got me the slipper, or an open hand. Bad days though…' Tyra's eyes appeared to become glossy for moment; she blinked a few times and they returned to normal. 'Bad days got me his belt, the broomstick, or just his fists.'

Danielle winced.

'But eventually there were more good days than bad. Less cuts and bruises, less crying. And the last day, I'll never forget.' Her eyes widened now, fire flickering inside them. 'Something changed in me that day. He was in my room for a full *hour*. It felt even longer…

'He threw everything at me, gave me bible passages to read, words I didn't even recognise. But somehow, I said them all, no stumbles, no mistakes…'

74

Tyra smiled proudly and admitted a prolonged pause. Danielle decided to break it.

'Then what happened?'

'He looked down at me and nodded. "Good," he said. "I've cured you." Then he left my room.' Tyra laughed loudly, which made Danielle jump; it was a harsh unmelodic kind of laugh. 'Anyway, he's dead now. Prick said I'd never graduate, but it looks like he was wrong about that. And, I g-got into Alabama State, so he can suck on that too.' Danielle smiled; much like a hostage trying to appease her captor. 'You won't be seeing me round here anymore. So, I guess this is goodbye.' Tyra squinted. 'Promise me something though…'

Danielle raised her head expectantly.

'Don't ever stay silent…Danielle.'

With that, the large girl strutted away, leaving the small one frozen in position.

She said my name, Danielle thought. *My actual name.*

Her mind automatically replayed a series of instances from the past couple years. Suddenly they all seemed completely different.

Spanish class exhibited all the symptoms of the last week before the summer break: freshmen were throwing paper airplanes, passing notes, handing them down the rows and laughing with abandon; the room was ear-splittingly loud, with no one paying the least bit of attention to anything written on the board.

Danielle was sitting on the back row, hunched over her desk. Although Mrs Fitzsimmons the Spanish teacher was desperately attempting to control her students, it resembled someone trying to herd thirty excitable rabbits into a tiny pen.

'All right, everyone. O.K., please. Everyone…*Quiet!*'

The noise lowered to a dull murmur.

'Now, I think each of you should get some practice for your oral exams. I will call you over one at a time…Danielle, you are excused—I have your note.' The teacher frowned. 'Although, I want you to know, I find this highly irregular.'

The teacher beckoned Danielle towards her desk. She walked over, ignoring the jeers and vile comments aimed at her on the way.

'Buh-buh-buh-bitch!' someone yelled, which received a moderate laugh.

She was an impenetrable wall though, and their significance was fading. One day she'd never have to interact with these people again—perhaps she wouldn't have to interact with anyone.

'As you're no longer busy,' Mrs Fitzsimmons said. 'I would like you to go to Mr Herbert's classroom, and give him this package…'

Danielle was handed an indiscriminate brown box. It had some weight to it.

Not at all happy with the request, she loped down the hall towards Mr Herbert's classroom with slumped shoulders, lessening her pace with each step.

The girl hadn't ventured to the room since submitting the infamous assignment several months ago, and she stood facing the door for a moment, wondering if she could get away with just leaving the box outside. Knowing it wasn't worth the hassle though, she let out a laboured sigh and knocked on the door.

'Come in,' she heard the teacher call out.

Mr Herbert was at his desk with Quentin Stevens sitting across from him. The two were laughing but quickly fell silent when Danielle entered.

'Oh, hello, Danielle. How are we?'

Danielle didn't answer but forced a weak smile of acknowledgement, then placed the box in front of him. Quentin watched her carefully as she did so.

'Ooh, I have an idea of what this might be,' the teacher said. 'How befitting that you're here, Quentin.'

Mr Herbert opened the box and removed a large gold trophy.

Quentin smiled.

As Mr Herbert proudly held up the cup, Danielle could just make out the inscription:

"National debate championships. 1st Place - Hopesprings High School"

'Yes, how wonderful—although, I can't believe how long we had to wait.' He grinned. 'This will take pride of place in the trophy cabinet. It's about time we had something to add to it!'

The teacher gleefully gestured to the lower inscription. 'And look, there you are, Quentin, immortalised forever.'

'Excellent,' Quentin said.

'I don't know if you're aware, Danielle, but Quentin here is the head of the debate team. And last year, his marvellous performance at the finals won our school its very first championship.'

Danielle nodded, expressionless. Her chest suddenly felt tight, however, and there was a dull ache in her gut, as if a blow had been delivered to it. The pain seemed deeper though, more residual, fading like a tender bruise.

'Yes. I see impressive things on the horizon for this young man. Are you still eying career in politics?'

'That's the plan,' Quentin said with a smug grin.

'Well, I think you've got a world of potential ahead of you.'

The feeling was akin to an out of body experience, like she was witnessing the scene from a separate pair of eyes. She also couldn't shake the sense of being subtly mocked; which, if not deliberate, was an impression unconsciously projected by the two men in the room and the significant detail they were deliberately not addressing.

It was possible that neither of them was truly cognisant of how sadistic the act was, of discussing Quentin's underhanded victory in front of her; they may have even assumed that Danielle was oblivious to the facts. In her mind though, this flagrant display was almost too sinister to bear.

She found it difficult to breathe and was almost grateful to the teacher when he said: 'Oh, that'll be all, dear. Run along'

June 23, 1998 (B.)

Danielle sat facing her Spanish teacher. Behind them the classroom was chaotic—the defiant overexcitement expected of a final lesson before the summer break: students were laughing and passing notes; paper planes and other crude projectiles were being launched across the room. And when she'd walked over for an impromptu end of year assessment, Danielle noticed that only a handful of textbooks were even open.

'Me g-gusta leer ciencia ficción y…e-estudiar en la biblioteca,' Danielle said, slightly breathless. Spanish was the only subject with a distinct oral element, and this had felt like the first formal test of her progress with Jarrell.

'Sí, Danielle. ¡Muy bien!'

The student felt a rush of relief. 'Gracias, Señora Fitzsimmons.'

The teacher beamed. 'Oh, wonderful. I am ever so proud…'

Danielle blushed.

'You say it's private speech therapy that's helped you?

She nodded.

'I really can't believe how much your verbal skills have improved.'

'Yo tampoco.'

The teacher chuckled. 'Maravillosa…' She ticked off a few boxes on a testing sheet in front of her.

'It's absolutely lovely to see, dear. Well, that'll be all… Don't forget to brush up on proper nouns over the summer holidays.'

'I will. Th-thank you.'

'Oh, actually.' The teacher suddenly raised a finger. 'Seeing as you're not going to get much done in this darned circus…' She glanced over Danielle's shoulder and tutted. 'I wonder if you might do me a favour? I signed for a package for Mr Herbert earlier, but I've been too busy to take to him. Would you be a dear and please pay him a visit? Here…' The teacher fumbled in her desk. 'I'll write you a hall pass.'

'Oh…Sure.'

Danielle carried the large brown box down the hall. She had a poised, determined look in her eye, like a conditioned sleeper agent suddenly deployed, awakened with a code word. With barely a pause at Mr Herbert's door, she gave it a resounding knock.

'Come in.'

She had hoped to find him alone—the classroom certainly sounded empty from the outside. When she entered, however, she saw him chatting jovially with a spotty senior. They'd never spoken, but she knew his name was Quentin Stevens.

'Oh, hello, Danielle. How are you?' the teacher said, slightly bemused.

'Fine, thanks,' she said brusquely. She raised the box. 'I was t-told to give you this.'

The teacher's bewilderment seemed to ease on discovering the reason for her visit. 'Ooh, I have an idea of what this might be,' he said with a covetous smile. 'Quentin, how fortunate that you happen to be here.'

Mr Herbert opened the package with a flourish and pulled out the large gold trophy from inside. 'Well, isn't this a sight for sore eyes…'

Danielle promptly piped up before the teacher could comment any further: 'That f-for winning the de-debate finals?'

'Oh…Yes, actually. Yes it—'

'Someone t-told me *all* about…that.' She forced eye contact with the teacher. He and Quentin shared a momentary look.

'Oh. Did they?'

'Yes. Apparently the ar-arguments were com-pelling.' She turned to the student. 'Now, Quentin, t-tell me…d-did you think of them all yourself?'

The senior shuffled awkwardly in his seat. 'Oh…I, er…Yes. Yes I think so.'

'Funny—and d-don't take this the wrong way—but someone m-mentioned…that your statements lacked *originality*.'

In spite of her very slight stumbles, Danielle asserted herself impeccably; she held continuous eye contact and set a swift, deliberate speaking pace.

'Well, you know, Danielle,' the teacher interjected, 'that's the thing about High School debating. It's often little to do with the words themselves, and more the way in which they're delivered. I mean, the arguments are often pulled from mainstream sources. Rarely are they particularly original.'

'That was the criticism I heard, actually,' Danielle pressed, refocusing on Quentin. 'N-No offence, but I was told you seemed quite robotic. L-Like you were just reading from a script…with n-no real c-connection to the words.'

Mr Herbert frowned. 'Nonsense. I don't know who you've spoken to, but Quentin here sounded perfectly natural. His delivery was strong.'

Danielle smiled, but it didn't quite reach her eyes. 'Oh, let's just drop the pretence, shall we? W-We we a-all know what you did to win that final.'

Cold silence.

Mr Herbert and Quentin locked eyes once more, clearly anxious for what she might say next.

'D-Don't worry.' Danielle smiled again. 'You can have it. I won't tell anyone.'

Mr Herbert and Quentin both squirmed in their seats, neither daring to speak.

'I just h-hope that wh-whenever either of you look at that thing'—she nodded at the trophy— 'or wh-when you think back to that cherished victory, you'll think of me. P-Perhaps you'll question why you had to rely on a ninth gr-grader to get the job d-done.' She headed towards the door but paused to turn back.

'It's scratched, by the way—top corner, ju-ust above the inscription.'

March 21, 2003 (A.)

Danielle sat in the rear section of the coffee house, silently studying. Like most days, she wasn't wearing make-up and her hair was tied up and messy. It made her appear younger than her actual age of 20. Various signs were scattered here and there, declaring 'Spring Break Deals' for students.

A moment later she looked up and her heart immediately began to race.

Announced by a small ring of the bell above the door, Quentin Stevens had entered with an unfamiliar female. It certainly looked like him, Danielle decided. But he was now free of acne, and his current haircut was a distinct improvement on the one he'd previously sported. If not for his teeth, which were as large and crooked as ever, he might even have been considered handsome. He found a table near Danielle without even paying her a fleeting glance; it was fair to assume he didn't recognise, or even remember, her.

The volume of his proceeding conversation was obnoxiously loud, enough for her to overhear every word.

'No! Did I not tell you? I'm doing my final year at Georgetown,' he proclaimed. 'I've been trying to transfer for the past three damn years and they finally accepted me.'

The girl beside him seemed demure and deferential—clearly a few years younger. 'Wow. That's really impressive…'

'To be honest,' Quentin said, maintaining his volume. 'I think it was the recommendation from my professor that swung it. He's actually a family friend…but I made sure he didn't reveal that to them.'

They both laughed.

Danielle scowled at them from her corner. It was hard to imagine disliking anyone more than she disliked her former Hopesprings alumni in that moment. It was a twisting, tightening kind of resentment, one that seemed to sap her of energy, filling her with listlessness and contempt.

Georgetown, she thought with bitterness, forcing herself to stop glaring at him; she'd once had designs on applying there.

While she didn't hate the way things had turned out, this almost forgotten dream stirred up stinging emotions. It reminded her how hopeful she'd once been, how ambitious.

Such aspirations now sounded laughable: the idea of studying in DC, finishing top of her class and becoming president.

Simplistic, lofty goals of a deluded child.

March 21, 2003 (B.)

Danielle was home for spring break. She wasn't quite sure why, but this morning she'd spent a considerable amount of effort on her hair and makeup just to study in a local coffee house. Perhaps it was the thought of bumping into someone from High School; she'd somehow graduated from Hopesprings in an enviable position, with her reputation miraculously transformed and her social-standing elevated beyond anyone's expectations—childishly, she clearly wanted to preserve this image.

The neighbourhood *was* small though; and just before she was about to enter, someone she vaguely recognised did pass by (though they looked too old to have been in her school year). While it forced her to do a double take, she still couldn't quite place them and carried on walking.

Clearly recognising her, however, the man turned back.

'Hey!'

Danielle stopped and faced him.

'You're Danielle, right?'

She nodded.

'It's Quentin, Quentin Stevens'.

Danielle slowly mouthed the name, still none the wiser, and the action left Quentin looking slightly embarrassed. He remained silent for a moment, and then said: 'We went to high school together. I was on the debate team…'

Realisation immediately dawned on her. He looked different now; his acne had cleared up and his haircut was far less unsightly.

'Oh. Hi, Quentin.'

'I, um, always hoped I might bump into you some day.'

Danielle nodded for him to continue.

'To be honest, I wanted to thank you.'

She was intrigued now. It suppressed the small swell of indefinite dislike she felt in seeing him again.

'My last day of school, you came into Mr Herbert's classroom…you must remember?'

The full memory came flooding back. She raised her head a fraction as she suddenly recalled the cause of her resentment. But unwilling to let on, she shrugged.

'Oh, man. Well…you just really put us in our place.' He laughed nervously. 'I…I'm sorry for going along with all that by the way—you know, the debate finals. When he handed me your assignment to memorise, I knew what we were doing wasn't right. But he was the teacher, you know…'

Danielle tilted her head back, slightly surprised by the apology.

'He told me to think of you as a ghost-writer. But it just felt so…shady.' Quentin shook his head. 'That day though, you telling us off like that, it was a turning point for me, a real confidence shaker—in the best way, I suppose. I was all set to do political science at college, but you made me rethink everything.'

'I see,' Danielle said.

'Anyway, my uncle is a bigwig at Blockbuster Video. And he set me up with a job. I'm store manager now, can you believe it? Making bank. And there's *real* career progression.'

'Good to hear,' Danielle said, wondering if he was going to try and sell her a membership.

'As a business, it's totally thriving. I've actually just bought a load of stocks.'

'That's cool.' Danielle smiled. 'Glad to hear you're doing well. And…no hard feelings, I guess. Apology accepted.'

Quentin looked thoroughly relieved. 'Thank you.'

She laughed. 'Honestly, it all seems like such a long time ago now.'

'For sure,' he muttered, looking down at his feet. 'Say, what are you doing these days?'

'I *am* actually studying political science. At Georgetown.' She said it offhandedly, as if the last detail were trivial.

Quentin's eyes widened. 'Wow. It looks like we switched paths! Not that I would have ever got into Georgetown. Hey, you don't have an uncle at Blockbuster too, do you?'

Quentin laughed and Danielle smiled awkwardly.

'Just kidding. Good luck with everything.'

'Thanks, you too,' Danielle said. 'Take care…'

She watched him for a moment as he walked away. There may have been a world where she'd hold an inflexible grudge for what he'd done to her at school, clutched it like a hot coal while absurdly expecting *him* to burn. It all seemed so insignificant now though, and seeing the man actually exhibiting remorse offered a sense of closure she'd never have thought possible.

You're not the bad guy, she thought with a faint smile; you're just a guy…

If the philosophy of Determinism had taught Danielle anything, it was the notion that there were essentially no bad people in the world—only bad actions. While this comforted her, such reflections often felt hazily abstracted, easier to abide in theory than in practise. Withholding blame and judgement *in the present*, when one party had clearly transgressed, was a tough skill to master.

But she decided it was something she'd work on it. For herself, more than anyone else.

Danielle was sitting in her cubicle in the Washington Post newsroom. At 23, she was one of the youngest journalists on the payroll; she'd had to fight tooth and nail to reach such a position, barely sleeping during the previous year, it seemed, becoming more used to the glow of computer screen than the daylight that occasionally crept through the blinds. Despite all this, it had still ended up feeling somehow hollow; journalism was, and would always be, a consolation prize.

For better or worse she'd grown into a gritty, all or nothing type of person: if she couldn't address scores of people with her words, she'd rather not speak at all; if she couldn't be a politician, she'd rather criticise them in the press. Although this presented obvious difficulties, coming this far with such a severe handicap was testament to her unshakable resolve.

She swivelled around in her chair to face Charlie, the Deputy Investigations Editor. He was accompanied by an intern perhaps a couple of years older than herself.

The editor addressed the intern: 'So, here's Danielle, the person you'll be helping—one of our very finest.' He smiled. 'This is great gig for you. You'll learn a lot from her.'

The intern shot Danielle a nervous glance. 'Hi. Nice to meet you.'

She nodded.

'She won't say hello back,' Charlie said, smirking. 'Don't take it personally.'

The intern seemed confused but said nothing.

Charlie laughed; he'd had to give the explanation several time before, and it now almost sounded rehearsed: 'This is essentially why you're here. You will be her voice. She'll do all the research, arrange the meetings and devise the questions. You'll simply be the one to ask them. She'll take all the notes and write up the piece. Easy money.'

'You, um, aren't paying me.'

Charlie chuckled. 'Oh yeah…Well, I'll let you guys get acquainted.'

The editor hurried away, leaving the young man standing in place, somewhat out of sorts.

'So, what's the story?' the intern eventually asked.

Danielle raised a finger; 'hold on', it indicated. She opened a large notepad page on her computer screen. Her typing was rapid, frenetic.

'It's an exposé on Quentin Stevens.'

It took the intern a moment to overcome this novel method of communication; he read her screen and then stared at her for a couple of seconds before he understood this was Danielle's authentic response. 'Oh…' he said. 'Who's that?'

'A newly appointed congressman with an extremely shady backstory.'

'O.K., great. What's our plan of attack?'

Danielle's reply was instantaneous, almost as fast as if she'd spoken it:

'Firstly, there is no 'attack'. He's going think we're writing a favourable piece on him, about his gaining a seat at such a young age.'

'Is that not a bit…disingenuous?'

Danielle smiled, then typed: *'Welcome to the big leagues, kid.'*

'Why him?'

'Because he's devious, arrogant, manipulative, morally reprehensible.' She paused at her keyboard for effect. *'And entirely capable of becoming president one day'.*

A few hours later the intern was sitting on the chair beside Danielle. He seemed considerably more comfortable with her now, and she with him.

'So, uh, how do you usually conduct interviews?'

'I get by,' Danielle typed. *'My situation is usually explained beforehand, and I either present them with pre-arranged questions, or someone like you asks them for me'.*

'I see.'

'But this time I want to try a different approach. You will simply state that you are conducting the interview to gain experience.' She tapped the caps lock key. *'DO NOT MENTION MY CONDITION.'*

'Um, O.K.…I don't really know what your…condition is. So consider that a promise.'

That afternoon Danielle and her new colleague were sitting in the office of Congressman Stevens. Quentin peered down at them from behind his desk in an expensive power suit. He was 26, with a smart crew cut and an immaculately contemptuous grin—his previously crooked teeth had evidently been replaced with a set of flawless veneers.

Danielle and the intern faced him. Their seats were markedly lower than his, she noticed.

'You see, it was my understanding that there would only be one of you undertaking the interview.'

Danielle remained silent, prompting her colleague to speak up.

'I'm on an internship. I need the experience. So, if it's all right with you, I'll be asking the questions.'

He seemed to consider this for a moment. 'Very well. Fire away.'

The intern briefly referred to Danielle's notes.

'O.K…You're widely considered one of the first congressmen to gain a significant internet presence, how does that feel?'

'It feels great, and I see it as a generational advantage; it's no news to anyone that as politicians go, I'm exceptionally young.'

He permitted a faint, self-satisfied smile before continuing.

'I feel like much of the public tend to regard us representatives as a bit out of touch, so it's great to be able to engage with people through these new mediums. The younger voters in particular.'

'Yeah. Your YouTube videos have garnered a lot of attention. And you've managed to amass hundreds of thousands of views for expressing what some would call quite controversial opinions. How would you respond to that?'

'Well, I'm candid. I say what I think, which I believe most people find quite refreshing.'

The intern pored over Danielle's notes.

'If we can talk about your campaign…How did you find that?'

'I enjoyed it. In my opinion any opportunity to connect with the public is a wonderful thing.'

'You certainly had a successful one…your, um, staff in particular seemed to have worked really hard. Were they paid well?'

Quentin briefly diverted his gaze from the intern to Danielle. 'They were rewarded fairly for their efforts, yes.'

'Oh, because there's talk that several of them are still waiting on payment…?'

Quentin's eye twitched, the only telling sign that he might have been irked by the comment. He otherwise gave the strong impression of someone wanting to appear entirely composed and calm.

'Oh no. I'm unsure what your sources are, but that's simply not true.'

The intern glanced at Danielle. She gave the nod for him to move on.

'You did have help from several prominent benefactors. Would you care to identify them, and explain your affiliation?'

'Oh, I rather think we have too little time and better things to discuss. They're out there. People can easily find them.'

The congressman suddenly drew his attention to Danielle.

'Hey, you look awfully familiar.'

Danielle's eyes betrayed her brief unease.

'Wait…' He grinned. 'Did you, by any chance, go to a crappy little school in South Texas by the name of Hopesprings High?'

Danielle's expression was inscrutable.

'Gosh, that's it. What an insanely small world! You tried out for the debate team once, right?' He paused, fixing his gaze on her. 'Yes!' he exclaimed, triumphant. 'You're the girl with the stutter, aren't you? …Do you remember Mr Herbert? He told me all about you; I heard you stopped talking entirely. Is that true?'

Danielle ignored Quentin, as well as the sudden acceleration of her heartbeat, and nodded at the paper in front of the intern.

'My colleague would like me to continue with the questions. You're the one being interviewed. Not her.'

The congressman beamed. 'Now this dynamic finally makes sense.' He feigned a sympathetic tone (which Danielle found utterly transparent). 'Oh, how unfortunate for you. It must be incredibly difficult trying to do your kind of work when you're a mute.'

Danielle returned eye contact with Quentin for a moment, then looked to the intern. She forcibly nodded, indicating for him to go harder; the young man raised his voice slightly.

'There are several sources out there that say you've misreported income, Congressman, as well as overstating expenses. And there are even rumblings of tax evasion. How do you respond to those accusations?'

'Ha! Well, I'd say anyone willing to accuse me of such crap better have the evidence to back it up.'

He shot to his feet.

'Now, I do apologise, but I'm afraid I've run out of time. It was lovely to chat to you *both*. My assistant will see you out.'

He reached over the desk to shake both of their hands. When gasping Danielle's, his grip seemed excessive, and he held on for a little too long.

'I'm certain we'll meet again, Danielle.'

October 11, 2006 (B.)

Danielle removed her long black jacket and hung it on a coat rack by her friend's front door. The apartment was cluttered with toys, but otherwise well-kept considering the distinct lack of space. On the wall was a picture of Tom, Lea's first and only partner, dressed in military uniform. A narrow hallway led onto a combined kitchen and living area.

Danielle sat down on an armchair in the far corner. Two twin boys, around 3 or 4 years old (she couldn't quite remember), were playing with monster trucks on the floor in front of her.

'You have your coffee black, right?' Lea yelled from the kitchen—her volume entirely unneeded given the proximity.

'Yes please.'

Though Lea was still only 24, she seemed aged beyond her years in the way young mothers sometimes become. Heavily pregnant, she waddled towards Danielle, handed her the coffee, and slumped onto the adjacent sofa.

'So, how you holding up?' Danielle asked softly.

Lea let out a long breathy sigh. She had prominent bags under her eyes, her hair was uncombed and wild, and Danielle noticed her shirt was inside out (a detail she decided not to mention). 'You know, taking each day as it comes.'

She peered over at her sons, whose playing had grown progressively louder since Danielle had entered; presently they were crashing their trucks into one another.

'Boys…' she said weakly, before quickly raising her voice. 'Boys!'

They stopped playing and both raised their heads expectantly.

'Why don't you go play in the bedroom for a little while, so mommy and her friend can talk?'

The boys nodded, gathered a handful of toys, and walked into one of the open rooms in the hallway.

'I'm sorry I haven't been back more,' Danielle said.

'No, I understand; you're extremely busy. You made it to the funeral—that meant a lot.'

Danielle nodded towards the hallway and lowered her voice. 'How are they doing?'

'It's hard to say. They were kinda used to him being away for long periods. I've had to remind them a couple of times…that he's not coming back.'

Unexpectedly, Lea broke down into quiet sobbing. Danielle reached forward to squeeze her hand, staying silent, deciding that her friend needed this brief release, far more than consoling words.

In ten years, this was the second time she'd seen her friend cry. The first was two months ago, at Tom's funeral.

'How are *you* doing…financially?' Danielle asked, when Lea had composed herself.

'Not great. The um…' she paused, 'death benefit wasn't great. I think because he wasn't killed in hostile action, and he only served for a few years. I—'

'He lost his life while serving his country.'

'Yeah, not as significant as it sounds, apparently.'

'Are you at least covered for now?'

'Mhm…' Lea nodded. 'I think when Tom Jr. is born though, I'll have to start thinking about going back to work at the bank. Mom said she can help out with childcare.'

'That sucks.'

'That's life.'

'It shouldn't be.'

Lea wiped her eyes and forced a smile. 'Yeah…can we talk about something a bit more positive? How are things with you, Miss Bigshot?'

'Good. I'm basically done with college, and I'm already starting to think about my campaign.'

Lea's eyes widened. 'For Congress? Already? But you're still so young.'

Danielle gave a half smile. 'So are you. And look at everything you're dealing with.'

Lea returned a feeble smile of her own. She looked as if she was about to well up again.

'I'm so fucking proud of you, Dani…I still remember that scrawny, frustrated little kid, with all the huge ideas and no way to express them. You never took your eyes off the prize, not for a second.'

'Yeah. I mean, I know it sounds corny, or pompous, or whatever…but I still want to change things. Still think I can.'

'You will. We'll be calling you Madame President before you know it.'

'Whoa. Let's…' Danielle smiled, pausing in fear that she might stutter (this only really happened now in moments of surprise or intense distraction). 'One step at a time,' she said.

November 4, 2008 (A.)

Danielle's apartment was sleek and modern, but seemingly lacking any sense of sentimentality or warmth. There wasn't a photo, or even an instance of artwork on any of the walls. She was now 25, sophisticated and mature in some respects, but incredibly callow and unworldly in others. She'd never had a boyfriend, and too few friends to mention.

She sat on her corner sofa, laptop open in front of her and a large glass of Malbec in her hand. Her current focus was on an all too familiar and irritating subject, Congressman Quentin Stevens. Perhaps hearing the former debate team captain regurgitating her words all those years ago, as if they were his own, had left her biased and overly critical; the deeper she'd dug though, the more troubled by him she'd become. Then, their meeting two years ago in his office had lit a fire underneath her, reigniting a hatred which probably served little purpose other than self-immolation.

Political journalism had become her life. And irrespective of whether she could verbally engage with her subjects, her comprehensive education (institutional and autodidactic) had made her an incisive, untiring reporter. Her mind was an unlimited hard drive of American politics. And while she knew every new development—from scandals to pieces of legislation— and every government official—ascending or descending, no matter how minor—it was fair to say that she'd taken an even greater interest in Mr Stevens's affairs.

She'd predicted it all: his explosion of approval, his elevation through the ranks, his amassment of deepened support—all won by playing on people's fears like a kind of bureaucratic vampire. Though he was still a couple of years shy of being eligible to run, Danielle could see 'Senator Stevens' as the logical progression for him, and perhaps even 'President Stevens' after that. She'd do everything in her power to try and prevent such a thing from happening. He had the charisma on his side now, the charm, and even a blindly loyal fan base.

Her clashes with the polarising figure had ramped up significantly in recent weeks. He was finally acknowledging her for what she was: a colossal thorn in his side and a serious threat to his future. She knew this from the online videos, which were rising in popularity. These frequent, attention-grabbing posts allowed him to address his public and attempt to silence any dissent. He seemed particularly keen to air his feelings of victimisation (from her, and at the hands of several other media outlets).

As the night drew on, the journalist watched video after video of him mentioning her by name—some of which had garnered millions of views. She was flabbergasted that a low-level politician could become so much of a celebrity.

She clicked and scrolled interminably, not needing to add another keyword. One video was titled '*Congressman Stevens destroys critics*', another was '*Brutal shutdown from Quentin Stevens.*' The one she lingered on longest, however, was titled '*Congressman Stevens calls out sly reporter*'.

She clicked play. Quentin was on what appeared to be a talk show, mid-interview. The host, whom she did not recognise, seemed amiable and overly receptive.

'So, Congressman. You're still incredibly young, but I imagine a run for the Senate is on the cards in the not-so-distant future?'

Quentin smiled his confident, veneer-sculpted smile.

'Seems like the way to go, doesn't it?'

'And can we expect to see *President* Stevens, after that?

'Well, safe to say, that's a long way off. But…if it's what the people want?'

Quentin laughed along with the rumble of applause this prompted from the studio audience. They were clearly buying into the desired narrative: young, ambitious politician from humble and blue-collar beginnings, clambering to breathe fresh air into a broken system.

'You certainly do have a following,' the interviewer said. 'Although, if you don't mind me saying, quite a few detractors too. I recall seeing a pretty scathing article about you in the Washington Post quite recently.'

Danielle tensed up.

Quentin was grinning, he shook his head slightly and sighed.

'Oh yes, I know the one. I've discussed this ad nauseam actually, but there is more than meets the eye with *that* particular smear campaign.'

'Do tell.'

'Well, funnily enough, Danielle, the young reporter who concocted that story, actually went to my high school.'

'You don't say…' The interviewer smiled widely at the revelation. 'So, would you call this a bit of a personal grudge?'

'Oh, there's no getting around it. That's exactly what it is.'

The host smiled. 'Refreshingly straightforward as usual, Congressman.' He leaned forward. 'If you don't mind delving a little deeper into that? We actually have an extract from said article. She wrote, and I'm quoting directly: "Mr Stevens has gained popularity by developing his own unique brand of hucksterism. A jarring combination of misdirection, showmanship and fearmongering that appears to compensate for his highly questionable character and obvious political shortcomings".' The interviewer paused and clenched his jaw. 'Yikes. How do you respond to that?'

Quentin chuckled. 'Well, I do wish she wouldn't hold back so much.'

The audience laughed and Quentin lapped it up.

'And I will simply respond in the same way I've done publicly, which is with this…' The politician turned to face the camera head on. 'Debate me, Danielle. Let's the two of us take to the stage and discuss these things like civilised people.'

He glanced across the studio audience.

'Wouldn't you all like to watch something like that?'

The audience cheered.

Quentin lazily gestured with his hand. 'You see, we all know what a unique opportunity it is that I'm proposing. How often are politicians so open to face their critics in a public domain?'

'Oh, so you've actually extended this offer to the reporter?'

'I certainly have. And I received a flat *no*.'

'And what was her reason for refusing?'

Quentin smiled like a Cheshire cat, then he looked down momentarily and shook his head. 'Her reason for refusing an open discussion is knowing that she will quickly be found out.'

Danielle's hand started to shake. Red wine sloshed around her glass. She stared with pure resentment at the deceptive figure on her screen.

'One should always be suspicious of this kind of keyboard warrior mentality. She can write a thousand essays detailing the so-called flaws in my ideas, as well as making—quite frankly—vicious personal attacks…' Quentin crossed his legs, leaning back, all too nonchalant. Then his voice took on a soft, silky quality. 'But the question is, if she won't take to the stage with me to discuss these topics like a civilised person, should anyone really give her the time of day?'

Danielle closed the video and promptly opened another one, followed by another, then another, well and truly descending down the rabbit hole.

She watched further enraging clips and skim read a plethora of related articles, all ultimately siding with him. Even his critics seemed to agree that she was cowardly for refusing his proposition.

In another video, Quentin was being interviewed outside City Hall.

'…This is a respectful request, Danielle,' the politician said casually. 'As I'm certain you'll see this. Let's talk it out. We can quite easily arrange a neutral audience and discuss all your reservations with me, or my policies. Let's be grown up about this and have a friendly conversation.'

A single tear tracked down Danielle's *right* cheek. He knew her situation full well; he knew without question why she couldn't do what he was asking.

She refilled her wine glass to the brim, closed her laptop, and got up.

Stumbling into her bathroom, she delved into her medicine cabinet, withdrawing several boxes of prescribed sleeping pills and Oxycodone. Then she returned to the sofa and emptied sleeve after sleeve of the pills onto her coffee table.

Several minutes later she began to hand write a note:

'This has been a long time coming. No true act of spontaneity.'

After stuffing a small handful from the indiscriminate pile into her mouth, immediately washing it down with the red wine, she continued writing:

'An old friend once told me that I had a wound. And my choices were to either treat it fast or leave it to fester.

One thing I've learned, however, is that there really are no such things as choices in this life. We like to think we are instrumental in the causal chain, when we are simply the resultant effect. All of us mere tools manipulated by an indifferent universe.'

Continuing to snatch at the pile of pills, Danielle opened another bottle of wine, and swigged directly from it.

Her writing quickly became less tidy.

'I know now that my wound was never destined to heal, and the only available path was the one I followed. Sadly, it would appear that this path has reached its end.'

Half an hour later the pile of pills had dwindled to almost nothing. She opened a third bottle of red and continued with the note, her writing now a barely legible scrawl.

'Presently my mind is flooded by concepts I've cherished since childhood. The 'Many Worlds Interpretation' is one such theory I've romanticised above all.'

She scooped up some of the remaining pills from the table, gagging slightly now as she swallowed. With some resistance, she forced the final two into her mouth and drained most of the last bottle, again dispensing with her glass. She struggled through her conclusion, her head spinning, her vision blurred (no nausea though; her stomach had always been strong).

'Perhaps there are infinite worlds. But this one will continue without me.

Sorry,

Danielle'.

She wrote the last with a laboured kind of flourish and slumped back onto the sofa.

November 4, 2008 (B.)

Danielle and Lea were side of stage in the packed-out hall. They had already exceeded capacity and security were now barring access, trying their best to prevent spill-over from the second mass of supporters forming outside. The combined volume of the two crowds forced Lea to shout at her old friend, despite only being a couple of feet away.

'Congratulations, Congresswoman.'

Beyond being music to her ears, the words struck her like the most stirring sonata; an injection of dizzying euphoria. 'Thank you,' she yelled back, laughing.

So many occurrences had led up to this single pivotal moment. A decade's worth of suffering and productivity, drudgery and exaltation. Recollections of the last decade seemed to replay themselves to her like a vibrant rapid show reel: skipping grades and topping classes; rejecting offers and recognising unwise shortcuts; choosing to stay in longer, more arduous lanes; always driving for what she held to be right, rather than what was easy.

Danielle grinned and pulled her friend into a powerful embrace. Each were holding glasses of champagne; she passed her own to Lea as she broke the hug, promptly smoothing down her dress.

Her face hurt from grinning as she shook each hand presented to her on the way to the stage. The joy of the announcement could not overcome her nerves, however, or the prospect of addressing her raucous audience, the noise of whom had doubled at the sight of her. There were network news crews in attendance; her victory was noteworthy, almost unprecedented.

She lowered the microphone on its stand and cleared her throat, standing there for a few speechless seconds.

'Th-thank you,' she finally said before admitting a massively pregnant pause.

'Such a beautiful welcome…' Danielle regained her breath. 'I cannot express the elation I feel as I stand in front of you all right now…'

She breathed heavily into the microphone.

'Despite such an extraordinary and truly humbling result, I know there must be some of you looking at me, perhaps examining my appearance for the first time, thinking: "Who is this child? Why do we want her representing us again? Have we made some grave error?"'

A small ripple of laugher fluttered through the rows.

'I am young, yes. But I think that all of us share the same vision. The very same purpose…we strive for a better, fairer future. We strive to support our families, and our friends. Some of us strive just to put food on the table.'

She was cajoled with a scattering of cheers and waited patiently for them to dissipate. All that remained thereafter was the now near-silent manifestation of obedience and intrigue.

'The shocking financial events of this year should teach us valuable lessons. And reflecting on this for a moment, I will tell you what we *do not* strive for… We do not strive for greed, for amassing wealth at the cost of the poor.' She broke into a yell. 'For bailing out corrupt organisations and fuelling this vicious cycle any longer!'

The crowd's initial enthusiasm to her taking the podium was matched with another eruption of resounding applause.

'I know you've heard this kind of rhetoric spewed a thousand times. So often that it's lost all meaning. There are those who have said it because they know it's what you want to hear. Because it's a way of winning an election. But I'm saying it because I know what it is to work hard. I know what it is to not be handed everything…I know what it is to struggle. These are lessons I will never forget.'

Danielle paused, this time for effect.

'You'll often hear the argument that struggle is good. It keeps us focused. It stops us from becoming complacent. And in many ways, I would agree. I think it's fair to say that it shapes many of us, it builds character and resolve. I can stand by that…'

She raised her voice a second time. 'But I'll tell you what I cannot stand by: the millions living paycheque to paycheque. The millions on welfare. The *millions* incarcerated because of the poor hand of cards they were dealt in life.'

The crowd's approval grew to a near ear-splitting level.

'Out there in this great country, I see deep division. I see disharmony and distrust. Just in this audience alone, I see a lot of very different faces. But no matter what we look like, no matter what kind of communities we identify with, or what ideas we cling to, we have far more in common with each other than you're often led to believe. And *far less* with any morally compromised bureaucrat or detached official, any clueless pen pusher, any civil servant who's forgotten that their role is to serve! These con artists who gained their position through lies and empty promises. We share nothing with them, and we share nothing with the *criminals* responsible for the avoidable crash we are now experiencing.'

More roars of approval ensued. Danielle beamed at her audience.

'There will be a lot of nervous people listening to this. People dedicated to maintaining the status quo. And I am here to tell you that *they are right to be nervous*. They are right to be scared. Because change is coming. Their days are numbered. This system…the one perpetuated to keep people down, to keep people *struggling* every day, is coming to an end…'

Her audience was irrepressible. Danielle waited for the clapping to die down, then deemed it necessary to carry on and shout over it.

'It won't happen overnight. And, I regret to say, it won't happen because of one person, like me. The change will come because we stand united!'

She took a few more measured breaths. Her conclusion was coming.

Stick the landing… she thought to herself.

Truly knowing our influence, we would never surrender our fate to the perpetrators of recent events, or the cold officials who were ignorant or complicit, or both. Truly knowing our influence, we would never *become them* when we experience some success.

Truly knowing our influence, we would build a future for *everyone*, not just for those rich enough to enjoy it!'

Danielle smiled. A single tear tracked down her *left* cheek as the support of her audience thundered through the hall, out onto the street. She stood there soaking in the moment, trying her best to enjoy this first crucial step towards her future, the reward of all her work and sacrifices: her fight to change things. While there was no guarantee that she ever would, it was empowering just to be in the fight at all. Over the next months, years, decades, she'd find out if her integrity could survive such an evidently broken system, or if she'd simply fold, as many had done before her. She had a feeling she'd be less pliable than most.

Despite her maturity, Danielle still held onto what some would regard as childish views, grand and almost inconceivable theories such as the 'Many Worlds Interpretation'.

Perhaps there were infinite worlds, she conceded, but *this one* was all that mattered.

Printed in Great Britain
by Amazon

40213948R00059